AF229510

REAP THE HOT SEPTEMBER HARVEST

Book 1: Desiree

Harry W. Kendall

Pen Culture Solutions
1-888-727-7204 (USA)
1-800-950-458 (Australia)
support@penculturesolutions.com

WE WILL NEVER FORGET

I wrote this novel in honor of the legion of courageous Freedom Riders. Their psychic energy kept the flame kindled in me while I studied their selfless contributions and carved out the story. Thank you, I plead for lack of a better way of expression other than my choice of words. They articulate my gratitude in acknowledging their perilous and supreme sacrifices.

Frances and Walter Bergman, Detroit MI
Albert Bigelow, Cos Cob CT
Edward Blankenheim, Tucson, AR
Benjamin E. Cox, High Point, NC
James Farmer, New York, NY.
Robert G. Griffin, Tampa, FL
Herman Harris, Englewood, NJ
Genevieve Hughes, Washington, DC
John R. Lewis, Troy, AL
Jimmy McDonald, New York, NY
Ivor Moore, Bronx, NY
Mae F. Moultrie, Sumter, SC
James Peck, New York, NY
Joseph Perkins, Owensboro, KY
Charles Person, Atlanta, GA
Isaac Reynolds, Detroit, MI
Henry Thomas, St. Augustine, FL
William Barbee, Nashville, TN
Paul Brooks, East St Louis, IL
Catherine Burks, Birmingham, AL
Carl Bush, Memphis, TN
Charles Butler, Charleston, SC

Joseph Carter, Brooklyn, NY
Alan Cason Jr., Orlando, FL
Lucretia Collins, El Pasto, TX
Rudolph Graham, Chattanooga, TN
William Harbour, Piedmont, AL
Susan Herman, Whittier, CA
Patricia Jenkins, Nashville, TN
Bernard Lafayette Jr., Tampa, FL
Frederick Leonard, Chattanooga, TN
Salynn McCollum, Snyder, NY
William Mitchell Jr., Oklahoma City, OK
Etta Simpson, Nashville, TN
Ruby Smith, Atlanta, GA
Susan Wilbur, Nashville, TN
Clarence Wright, Nashville, TN
Jim Zwerg, Beloit, WS

Among the list of more than four hundred Freedom Rider champions for justice, these thirty-eight were victims of the Mother's Day, April, 1961 massacre in Anniston and Birmingham, AL. They were onboard the Trailways and Greyhound buses. Their valor inspired me to name the protagonist in Book I, *Desiree*. To Ye Scribe she personifies beauty, love, strength of spirit, and indomitable perseverance.

Reap the Hot September Harvest

Book 1: Desiree

Harry W. Kendall

ENDORSEMENTS

Harry Kendall in *Reap the Hot September Harvest* deftly navigates contested contexts of time, space, and place with the precision of reported observation and storytelling of a community's griot. We are enriched within and through these iterative moments, narratives of and as movement(s) passed across more than 60 years, and long before that, and across physical, song- and spirit-filled, and social geographies collectively tracing and bearing witness to a corridor of simultaneous hope and the hoped-for from the Deep South to Philadelphia, Pennsylvania, and back. Kendall compels us at once to travel and dwell, to sojourn with this historicizing, acutely necessary in our contemporary time: he writes stories with a Black literary and African Diasporic tradition of authors who locate us alongside characters and in texts spanning powerful genres of prose, song, and the historical present to envision possibilities in the interactions of equality, action-taking, and love, expressed intergenerationally as individual and collective imaginaries of lives lived and complicated in desires for envisaged pasts, presents, and futures, and in outcomes unanticipated.

Dr. Vaughn W. M. Watson
Assistant Professor of English Education, Michigan State University

In part love story, in part a deep felt reflection on the painful milestones of the civil rights movement, Harry Kendall's *Reap the Hot September Harvest* is ultimately a novel of ideas—an erudite and compelling mediation on the path from oppressive religious practice to true spiritual freedom.

J.E. Fishman
Author of Primacy and Dark Pool

Reap The Hot Harvest September takes you on an exciting and historical journey from the rural south to the land of the pyramids. Kendall reaches beyond civil rights activists and historians in this book.

Ernie Wade PhD
Former Director of Multi-Cultural Affairs Wake Forest University

ACKNKOWLEDGMENTS

Writing this novel has been a metaphysical odyssey. More so than writing holistically as the thought processes meshed, its demand never ceased that I rise spiritually in sync with the story's arc. I still hear those voices appealing for a sustaining level of intellect though ever mindful of simplicity. I could not have completed this work alone. Thank you Alma Hairston, Robert Garwood, Joel Fishman, Susan Hacker, Gary Smith, Dorothy Graham Leverett, Judith Burgess, Lieutenant Commander Cheryl Hawthorne Human Resources Officer U. S. Navy, Karen Duran, Mitchell Kendall, Dr. Ernest Wade Professor Emeritus Wake Forest University.

Without the solid support system—my wife, Shirley Sharp-Kendall, Marie Tommasini, Denice Waite, Gertrude Simmons, and Scott Allen—I would have achieved very little beyond the first draft. Thank you for bolstering me with the confidence to stay with my original decision. Write this historical perspective and its projection as a work of fiction.

Grateful recognition is made to Dr. Mervat Nasser, Founder and Director of New Hermopolis and the Djehutihotep Cultural Center, for use of copyrighted material in the World Memory, the Corpus Hermeticum, and the photo of Tehuti.

BOOK ONE

I, thy God, am the Light and Mind, which were before Substance was divided from Spirit and Darkness from Light. And the word that appeared as a pillar of flame out of the Darkness is the Son of God, born of the mystery of the Mind. The name of the word is Reason. Reason is the offspring of Thought. Reason shall divide the Darkness from Light and establish Truth in the midst of waters. Understand, Oh Hermes, and meditate deeply on the mystery. So it is that Divine Light dwells in the midst of mortal darkness, and ignorance cannot divide them. The Union of the Mind and the World produces the mystery called Life... Learn deeply of the Mind and its mystery; therein lies the secret of immortality.

Meditation of Tehuti (ancient Egyptian scribe) on immortality

CHAPTER 1

Shades of Honor

May 14, 1961

Early on a clear and balmy Mothers' Day Sunday, Desiree Pierson, an eighteen-year-old Temple University sophomore and other Freedom Riders, mingled with a hundred-fold crowd at Atlanta's bus depot. Mostly black and white college students, professors, and teachers were members of CORE, the Congress of Racial Equality. With the anxious bunch, CORE waited in a cordoned area with two cross-country buses for the arrival of Reverend Martin Luther King, Jr., and James Farmer.

Desiree, five feet five and ideally proportioned with sharp cheekbones and elongated brown eyes in a narrow face, had been standing there for hours, believing it would all be worth it. She wore a faded long-sleeve working man's shirt and blue denim jeans. Desiree shifted her stance, trying to get more comfortable, as she shielded the bright Georgia sun from her eyes, and peered ahead. Suddenly a loud whoop resounded. Pride and excitement rose in her heart. She, along with the others, clamored for position in the jammed area, close enough to touch approaching Reverend King and Mister Farmer, CORE executive director.

Not a tall man, of medium built, and mahogany complexioned with a thin mustache, intensely clear black eyes, and close-cropped hair, Reverend King held the admirers in awe. He wore a gray, blue and black cotton polo shirt, and dark blue trousers.

Desiree stood directly in Reverend King's path. Their eyes met. His held an expression that signaled to Desiree, that if she was indeed bold enough to meet his gaze he would smile.

He did. "You are an instrument of God's will. Hold tight that trust, proud young lady." Reverend King's baritone voice resonated in Desiree's entire being. At once, the center of his attraction, she nervously adjusted the bill of her Homestead Grays National Negro League baseball cap. Like Desiree, the others were mesmerized by the baritone resonance in his voice. It would rise and descend as if carried by gentle wind currents to everyone he greeted. Desiree felt exceptionally noble and secure in Reverend's King's presence.

Mr. Farmer, a huge athletically built and balding man in a white polo shirt and gray denims, followed the Reverend smiling, joshing and encouraging riders for the trip they were about to start. Himself a minister, and the backbone of this CORE project, Farmer had years of experience, which had begun years earlier as a co-founder of a lesser-known civil rights organization, the Journey of Reconciliation.

Cracking silly jokes, forcing joviality, he led a group of riders to the Greyhound bus. The others surrounded Reverend King, going to the Trailways. Suddenly, a car, swerving as it roared into the station, sent all of them scurrying. "Stop!" Farmer yelled.

Two men jumped out, nodding grimly, and waving their arms. CORE scouts they were, calling out to him. Farmer summoned Reverend King. As they conversed, anxiety contorted Farmer's face. Observing them, uneasiness began circulating among the riders. After several minutes of an obviously grim conversation, the scouts left. Farmer returned to the Greyhound.

Reverend King in his usual contemplative manner, left arm across his chest, right hand stroking his chin, stared at the scene around him. He returned to the Trailways, his face devoid of expression. Looking directly at Desiree, she being obviously one of the youngest travelers, he suggested she might reconsider the grave seriousness of this leg of their journey.

Desiree forced her lips into a stiff smile, waiting for an explanation to what had made the journey graver than already anticipated. Reverend King stared and blinked as if at a loss for words. Worry distorted his perspiring face. Desiree, head-strong and made courageous by earlier encounters on their trip from Washington, DC, addressed the stalwart giant of a man. She reminded him of her fervent dedication, not unlike his. Absorbed in obvious fear, Reverend King responded resolutely to the hushed busload, that he would not go to Anniston, AL, with them. The dreaded Ku-Klux-Klansmen were waiting. Jail would be a certainty.

He probably would not leave there alive. Desiree, as well as the others, stared aghast at him. Reverend King beseeched the bus driver not to desert them.

Paul Kulaks, a young athletically built white pre-medical student from Cornell University sitting beside Desiree, heaved a long audible sigh.

The reverend heard someone call him a spineless coward and dodging a big fight. His quiet answer—a prayer Desiree barely heard—for God to affirm the civil rights leader's faith that He would protect them. Come evening, whether tragedy came to any or all, they would be tomorrow's heroes and heroines. The world would record their day's work at trampling sanctioned fascism Southern style, a fascism that had counterfeited the United States' Constitution.

In departing, he praised the busload for their unyielding valor and courage, though Desiree noted, no one said goodbye. She wrote in her journal, *to my next of kin,* in close, small words along with her name, address and phone number. After tearing the bit of paper and folding it neatly, stuck it deep inside her brassiere. Then she pulled her hair tightly into a bun, secured it with an elastic band, and tucked it underneath her cap. Other women on board did the same. Paul and the other men checked identity cards in their wallets or stuffed bits of paper into watch pockets of their dungarees.

#

CHAPTER 2

Gandhi's Principle, First Line of Assault

May 14, 1961

Passengers aboard the Greyhound similarly prepared themselves. Farmer had warned them, angry mobs were waiting about one hundred miles down the road in Anniston. Unfortunately, he had just received news that his father had died, and he must hurry to Washington, DC.

"That figures." A voice rang out from the back of the bus. Farmer didn't answer. He asked for a vote to cancel the trip. An elderly Black woman, the oldest person in the group, began singing a Negro spiritual.

I shall not, I shall not be moved.

Like a tree planted beside the water,

I shall not be moved.

The answer to Farmer, an emphatic no, followed by resounding cheer. Just as he prepared to leave, a young woman whom he doubted weighed more than one hundred pounds grabbed his arms, her wet eyes imploring. "Please James."

Farmer's lips quivered. He looked out the window, whistled at the challenge to his conscience and heard himself quoting Gandhi, *I would rather have a man resist injustice with violence than fail to resist out of cowardice.* He promptly sat directly across from the driver, thinking he might very well join his Dad in that "great getting up morning," when all the saints would gather at home. Three cheers rang out from the crowded Greyhound as it pulled away, the first to leave.

Tall, lean with a chiseled face and a prophet's beard, James Peck, tried-and-true CORE associate of Farmer's, stood and adjusted his glasses. "The eyes of the world are on us, crusaders of non-violence against violence, justice against horrors born of injustice. Our line of assault is passive resistance, our only defense. We are the Constitution's legionnaires of triumph over segregation." James challenged each rider to state why he or she was so hell-bent on routing the demon from his domain.

The woman who had led them in song answered first. "I'm tired of carrying Mississippi Samsonite—shoe boxes packed with food—and having to relieve myself alongside the road. Or in filthy holes called colored toilets." A somber quietness spread throughout. She though, restored the fake joviality. "Feeding wayside rats and dogs with the chicken bones we pitch out the windows all the way from here to Washington."

They clapped and laughed for an hour or so, as others recalled similar indignities, building determination and camaraderie. Their driver read aloud the sign over his intercom, announcing their entry into Alabama. Laughter waned, as the crusaders in the Trailways watched the Greyhound, bound for Birmingham, speeding away.

#

CHAPTER 3

Driven by Blind Madness, The Crucible

May 14, 1961

Even with air-conditioning pumping cold air into the Trailways, Desiree's lightweight spring clothing clung to her skin. Obvious wet patches of perspiration embarrassed her. Sitting without fidgeting was extremely difficult. Paul wiped his neck with a big red and black workman's handkerchief. He had slipped off his shoes. The odor of feet sweating in athletic socks rose up around him. He and Desiree offered each other a sheepish, understanding smile.

There were many trips back and forth to the toilet. An hour later, the driver said they were coming into the Anniston, Alabama bus depot, a thirty-minute Trailways rest stop.

Paul cleared his throat. "Just being here," he said, off-handedly, "means you gotta have the heart of a giant."

"Speak for yourself, big guy." Desiree offered him a humorous and wide-eyed look.

The bus slowed, turned into the station, and stopped. An eerie silence prevailed, neither stray dog, a Saturday night left over town drunk, nor a waiting passenger. Too uncommon for that Sunday morning transportation terminus.

"Lookit." Paul glanced at Desiree. "I mean, if things get real ugly, curl up in your seat. I'll cover you."

His sweating fingers rubbed Desiree's hands nervously. "Maybe I'll need to cover you, Mr. Giant." Then, honking vehicles pulled up behind and beside the bus. Her left hand interlaced with his right. He squeezed so tightly, Desiree felt her joints crunch. Pandemonium! Like attack dogs, yelling and cursing hooded men armed with chains, pick handles and bats, broke windows, hammered the bus, and slashed at its tires. The back door flew open; marauders rushed in and began mauling their way to the front. The driver quickly opened the front door. Some screaming Riders fled, as they and others were yanked from the bus and attacked.

"Curl up!" Paul pushed Desiree down and flung his long body over her. Cowered into a ball with her arms wrapped around her head, every assault made him heavier and heavier. He felt like an eleven-hundred-pound cow lying on her. Reaching under Paul, a goon grabbed her arm, scratching as he yanked and tugged. Terrified screams rose up from her, just as pistol shots rang out. Two policemen came on board, chased the terrorists from the bus, and yelled to the driver. "Close the door and get the hell out of here." They left and guided him into the street.

Crumpled under Paul's limp body, Desiree began convulsing. Amid uncontrollable spasms, and struggling for air, she felt herself losing consciousness. Then, she slipped into darkness.

Reverend Fred Shuttlesworth, a slender mahogany man with bright, bespectacled eyes in a small round face, arrived with a cavalcade of armed black rescuers. As they leaped out, long guns pointing, the police with bullhorns threatening arrest, demanded the mob disperse. Some rescuers came onboard and helped the delirious and injured travelers. Others searched the area until they had rescued every person, many who were traumatized and reluctant to return.

Desiree found herself at the distant shore of some lake she had never seen. Her rag doll, a companion her mother took from her at eight years of age, was lying at the water's edge beside a canoe. She pushed the boat into the water, green with algae and smelling like fish. Desiree climbed in, and clutching the doll between her legs, she paddled with one oar. The farther she moved from shore, the clearer the water became, until it was sky blue with only a tint of the seaweed. A current propelled the canoe across white-capped waves, toward a shoreline. Desiree saw herself coming upon an islet, on which sat a medieval-style stone castle built right down to the water's edge. A high, rusting wrought-iron fence surrounded it. Waves lapped the shoreline in a rhapsodic monotony. The current rushed Desiree and her doll through a narrow and dark descending canal. At the bottom, she floated into a chamber filled with a pale emerald light. A short, heavy-set nurse, wearing white hosiery on her thick legs and singing as she came upon Desiree, tried to snatch her doll. Desiree, though much smaller, held fast. A sudden gust of wind whisked her and the doll upon a table in a doctor's office. Harpsichord music pervaded. The authoritative voice of a surgeon just beyond the margins of a blinding light beaming on her, interrupted the melody.

"Her will is too strong," he advised, "let her keep it. A case of eudemonic frenzy it seems to me, a throwback to Civil War times among, shall I say, certain people with warped minds?"

He sounded like a Dixie bigot twanging in a long Swiss alphorn. Desiree struggled in that dense twilight zone to make sense of it all.

"She is caught-up in that suicidal train of thought like some other retarded, evil children of Satan before her."

In the next moment, she sensed him up close barking, though in a whisper. "Strapping a human time bomb across your shoulders, antagonizing genteel white folk, forcing the world to view us as demented bigots. No sane Christian would ever attempt that."

Desiree felt a needle injected into her arm. "This should settle her," he said.

Floating and completely free of pain, Desiree slipped into a peaceful darkness. Hours later, she awakened in the bed of a segregated local hospital, swathed in gauze and bandages. A staring nurses-aide, dabbing medication to cuts about her head, neck, and body, tried to determine if Desiree was crying or laughing. She raised Desiree to a sitting position and steadied her. A nurse rushing about stopped long enough to put a tiny white pill in Desiree's mouth. Tilting her head back, the nurses-aide poured a swallow of water between Desiree's slightly parted lips.

She gulped and nodded her head for another swallow. Desiree gazed with weak, half-shut eyes at the woman holding her and asked if her comrades were dead. But mumbling through parched and swollen lips, the aide couldn't understand her. Sleep came suddenly and stayed with Desiree a long time.

The next day, while feeding Desiree broth and water sweetened with honey, the aide said the FBI feared she might have been kidnapped. She had seen Desiree's picture on national television. United States Attorney General, Robert Kennedy had ordered Alabama's National Guard to Montgomery, and the Mississippi State Police had been ordered, she said, to escort the Freedom Riders to Jackson. Desiree called the names of some of her comrades, David Kulaks, Moses Newton, Genevieve Hughes, Edward Blankenheim, Mae Francis Moultrie, and Clancy Lake, a radio newsman. Her voice trailed off to a mumbled whisper. Desiree began sobbing. Some people whose names she mentioned, the nurses-aide had seen. But she wouldn't know about the white ones. They wouldn't be in the colored ward. Desiree read the extreme sadness in her eyes, and suspected that whatever she wouldn't reveal was tragic.

"Is it real bad?"

The aide tenderly squeezed Desiree in her warm, plump arms. "Reverend Shuttlesworth spoke to your mama. She and your papa's flying down to fetch you home soon's you can travel." The aide told Desiree the Reverend would be coming shortly to discharge her from the hospital. She was a national celebrity and being alone without security put her in grave danger.

Within the hour Reverend Shuttlesworth came and bending over Desiree, he touched her forehead. She asked him about her friends. Word had spread by way of the network, he told her, their section of Alabama was overrun with beaten and bewildered Freedom Riders fleeing the peckerwood. He read the question in her face and explained. "Peckerwood, more than a name, is an earned description of all that is perverse about conceived despicability. It is a perversity, like a balloon-eyed sea monster that lurks in the midnight fathoms of the Gulf of Mexico. It surfaces and regurgitates a wall of fiery destruction, and then dives back to its haunt. Direct rays of a penetrating sun, having hard-boiled its brains, had driven it to blind madness."

#

CHAPTER 4

Nearer My God to Thee

May 18, 1961

Desiree screamed at the forlorn whistle of a freight-train diesel engine; the clickety-clack-clack of its iron wheels so close she tried rolling out of bed to avoid them. But the little white pill held her immobile on an iron frame cot in the back room of a tiny log house beside a single railroad track. The slight and bald elderly man in flannel pajamas looking down on her, appeared ghostly in Desiree's cloudy vision. Just the four-forty a.m. switch engine hauling lumber from the sawmill down the line a ways, he assured her. Malachi Moses, Uncle Mal he suggested Desiree call him, would protect her. His wife, Aunt Grace would make her well enough to travel. With unsteady fingers, Mal adjusted the wick of an oil lamp, making a bigger onyx shadow of himself on the dark wall, and quietly called his wife. Bed springs in an adjoining room creaked. Aunt Grace, short and rather plump and looking as if she could be Mal's sister, pulled aside a panel of drapery hanging in the doorway.

"It's a mite chilly." Aunt Grace fumbled with the top button of her lengthy granny-gown. "Stoke the fire, Mal." She crossed the floor to Desiree's bedside, her bare feet slapping the brown linoleum, its lines of trapezoids and elongated circles extending from the center to its darker border.

Aunt Grace looked deeply into Desiree's swollen and frightened eyes. "Get my glasses," she whispered to Mal, and folded her arms across her breasts. "This child needs a heap of attention."

They were deep in timberland Klan country, she explained to Desiree, a long ride to Birmingham and too close to Anniston. Aunt Gracie would be pleased if Desiree just rested quietly, as she had done since arriving yesterday afternoon. The doctor would come later in the day. She and Mal heard it on the air that federal marshals had escorted the Freedom buses to Montgomery.

Could she, Mal asked, so young and innocent looking, do all they had heard on the radio, stoking the fire in Dixie's cracker-dom hell? From the very moment that Reverend Shuttlesworth had asked him to hide Desiree, Mal had been uneasy. Aware that he couldn't say no, but doubtful that it was a sound decision. He shook his head distressfully at reoccurring thoughts that plagued him.

The hard reality of Desiree's pain, spurred by answers to Mal's questions about her commitment to the equality struggle, began clearing up some of her confusion. She was at their mercy in that backwoods haunt. Percolating coffee, the crackle and pop of burning wood and salt pork frying, relaxed her knotted stomach a bit. It growled acceptance to Aunt Grace's tasty, hot broth.

"She needs to get up. Go make the fire a little hotter, Mal, and fill the tub half full."

"Ever bathe in a galvanized tub?" Aunt Grace nodded acceptance to Desiree's whispered no, and humorless smile. As Desiree slipped from beneath the covers, Aunt Grace batted her eyes, and momentarily turned away while wrapping the quilt around her. "Yes indeed, you gettin' a nice hot bath today, young Miss."

On wobbling legs, with Aunt Grace helping, Desiree stepped into the water, especially hot to her toes and buttocks. From head to toe, Aunt Grace scrubbed firmly, though gingerly, while Desiree winced at the touch to bruised and tender places in her anatomy.

Several days later, the caring couple noticed the pain in Desiree's eyes receding. In its place, Grace noted an indescribable emotion brimming with anger.

"God," she pleaded, "bless this child's mom with the mother wit to know her daughter's been hit by an earthquake. Have mercy on both of 'em, sweet Jesus."

Hearing her, a defiant Desiree lifted her arm and clenched her weak fist into what would become the black power symbol. Unwittingly, she provoked a disturbance to Mal's moral conviction. A conviction that he, a rugged black warrior of WWII, had finally become able to soothe enough to live relatively peaceful.

"She got no business here." He bit his lip savagely and looked down.

"Where else can this poor, beat-up child go?"

"I should' a told Shuttlesworth naw, she can't stay."

"But you didn't so stop frettin.'" Aunt Grace gnawed on her thoughts then asked, "What's chewing on you?"

"She's a haint."

"Lordy, Mal. She's been boggered up but is a long ways from dead."

"Just keep her away from me."

"She can barely walk, that won't be hard."

Desiree couldn't hear what she imagined was small talk, though she noticed the trembling in Mal's arms when he went outside.

Standing in the doorway, self-consciously distressed, he called out to Desiree, "It looks like a right nice day coming on."

Desiree didn't answer, even though the gloomy room that protected her from the hostile outside world seemed menacing. When Mal disappeared, Aunt Grace moved Desiree near the window.

Every day for several weeks she sat God-like in the healing sun watching, though unmindful that she reminded Mal of his shame. Even though Desiree was not afraid of Mal, she maintained a psychic distance between them. Watching him with his head hung low, and wander alongside a distant creek that glistened like a sheet of glass, she wondered. What was there about her that was so bothersome to him? Then she would fall asleep.

#

CHAPTER 5

The Blues Nth Expression is a Good Man Loathing Himself

May 21, 1961

Mal had been forced by Desiree's presence to dwell on what disturbed him to admit. Sixteen years, since his gallant return from Italy in '45 with the Ninety-Second Infantry Division, he had lived in a vacuum. Well, not all sixteen, but enough for him to discount the several earliest years living too high on Cloud Nine. He had tramped around in the chitt'lin circuit with a rhythm and blues septet after returning from Europe. Mal read the virtuous conviction, which he knew so well, deep in Desiree's eyes. They reminded Mal of the Italian village girls crouching alongside him in the Alpine Mountains with bullets whizzing inches above his head. Desiree, like them defying death, had infiltrated Dixie's badlands fighting peckerwoods fire, and dynamite with nothing except the driving force of her soul. Dammit!

She was forcing him to reexamine those contradictions from which he had run. Fighting a war and returning to a hell that was worse in many respects than when he had left. It was certainly worse than anything encountered by the Buffalo Soldiers 370th Combat Team. Desiree made him remember what he had worked so hard to deny in the deep pocket of his conscience. He vividly recalled, while on board the troopship feeling anxious to face enemy Germans and Italian Fascists. Black troops were finally given live ammunition some thousands of miles away from American shores. It really wasn't in Mal's heart to kill or punish and leave writhing in agony. At the time though, he believed life under Hitler and Mussolini would probably be worse than American racism, and he understood that in war, killing was inevitable.

The stark truth made an indelible impression in his first close-up encounter. Buffalo soldiers had advanced through thick woods and the minefields of Viareggio, some ten miles north of Pisa. Across the Arno River they battled up the slopes of Mount Pisano against Nebelwerfer fire. Rockets slamming into the mountain, raining down boulders, and dirt, buried Mal up to his neck. Civilian Italian men and women, spurred to action by his platoon routing the enemy from their locale, helped them dig out from their foxhole tombs. Mal came upon a wounded boy just about Desiree's age lying on the ground. Mal read the question in his blood-soaked eyes before he spewed at him in broken English. "Why would you, of all the goddamned black fools on earth, do this to me?"

Then seeing the boy desperately trying to aim his gun, Mal pointed and fired, though his gun went off a split second after someone close behind him had fired. He turned around and saw a girl trailing close behind who had saved his life. After that, Mal made it his business to aim straight for the heart, never yielding to cries from men he might have wounded to spare them or take them prisoner, for no other reason than to save himself from their slaughter. Yet, in his heart Mal felt pain, though he couldn't explain why to himself and wouldn't try explaining himself to another person. The yoked guilt he held made him worse off. Mal, returning home after the war weighted with those convictions, soon learned that despite all that he had done for liberty's sake, it is still denied him. In Italy, he had been exalted. In Alabama, hatred for black soldiers worsened. If anyone of them—a Kraut, a Dago Fascist, or an Alabama peckerwood—had killed him, he wouldn't even have been mourned.

In an attempt to release severe and mounting anger without getting himself in serious trouble, he began singing. A natural down-home blues shouter, Mal bellyached humorous dissatisfaction in a most raucous way. It was about not only all that he found perverse and deceitful down Dixie-way, but throughout America.

Yes, he fed the hungry souls of angry men, patriots destined to become jailbirds. He hazarded the urban wilderness of America's Sodom's and Gomorrah's, doing one nighters while entertaining former GIs who had scoffed at doom, men with iron guts who could have been Oxford scholars. Too many had become Harlem hepcats, Baltimore jive Maryland farmers, Philly mammy jammers, Motor City studs, Fifty-fifth and Cedar alligator-shoes wearing Cleveland daddy-os, hip-kiddies of Pittsburgh's Herron Hill. In Atlanta, Chicago, Birmingham, Los Angeles, St. Louis, or Memphis, no matter what ghetto the story was the same. Living in roach dives with their big city broads, sniffing nose candy and other mind-bungling shit. Rejecting the white supremacists stepsons, Holy Willie the hypocrite and Jim Crow, in the vilest way humanly possible. Mal's was a voice speaking clearly with a brand of blues that Johnny, who had come marching home amid the ticker tape and unfurling of Old Glory, couldn't duplicate.

Yet, the despicable and unbridled appraisal of joy versus sadness and rage opposed to happiness, hate crushing love and lusting passion for the moment's thrill could not stay the undercurrents of hard-core wrath. A wrath, fueled by so many heroes in Europe, dethroned to disenfranchised ugly patriots upon returning to America. The Blues, though in all of its unencumbered examination and its appeal to thousands, could not ward off that rejection. Even Mal, rising in stardom, grooving high with big swing machines and meshing his brand of blues with the jazz giants in Bop City, did not channel the rage. While he and the giants began shaping a genre with an academic attractiveness and sophistication, the nightmarish influx of more liquor, heroin, and its associated gook turned the streets into war zones. The degeneracy of it all tore at Mal's nerves. It got worse as the years wore on.

Hustling past a little church in Wheeling, West Virginia on his way to a gig one Saturday evening, Mal heard a voice that compelled him to stop. It was Little Richard, of all people, inside preaching. It seemed as if the former blues shouter was directing his message at him. Mal went straight away home to Dixie, hung up his guitar, gargled the blues-gravel from his throat, and picked up his Bible. Mal absorbed himself in preaching hellfire in the same manner he had screamed the Blues. He carried cement on his shoulders—a hod carrier by day, who did extra work dipping honey from old toilets at night. He concentrated his study in the book of Malachi. That made Grace and his deceased mother happy, he had reasoned.

Thinking back, it might have been a joke he played on himself in the peckerwood's world. Perhaps not. For certain though, country preaching insulated him from the urban scourge. Even if it required some yezzabossing, bowing and scraping the floor for Holy Willie and Jim Crow, he did not dishonor any woman, man, or child again in thought, word, or deed. Now, settling into his last years, he reckoned that this angel of mercy had ended up smack dab in his refuge. A tender blossoming spring flower, its chaste black centers not yet turned red by the bees sucking its sweet nectar, had punched a hole in his invisible shield. Desiree was forcing him to see again, the ugly from which he had scampered, rather than fight. Now he was too old to run. Where could he hide? Its prophecy—reality he may as well accept as written in the Book of Malachi, the last prophet of the Old Testament: *The Lord will come to judge and purify his people, sending ahead of him his messenger to prepare the way.*

Mal accepted his fate. Desiree was the messenger.

Late that night Mal took his shotgun and walked downstream beyond view of his home. He stood a long time by the noisy bend in the creek, facing the hard, cold reality of himself. An old Alabama nigra who had retreated from the home-front lines. They should have meant more to him than all the combined battles he had fought in Europe. Under the eerie light of a crescent moon, Mal watched water cleanse the stones as it rushed over them. He listened to the sucking sound a deepening whirlpool made flushing up dirt from the bottom and thought about Grace washing away Desiree's stains of ugliness. She would go back to her folks in Birmingham or Mobile.

He wrapped a towel loosely around the hammer and eased into water up to his neck. Extending his arms with the fingers crooked rigidly around the trigger above water, and the barrel end under water against his chest, he squeezed.

> Yet I hope, still I long to live.
> And if there can be returning after death
> I shall come back. But it will not be here.
> If you want me, you must search for me
> Beneath the palms of Africa. Or if I am not
> There you may call to me across the shining dunes.
> Perhaps I shall be following a desert caravan.

Arna Bontemps-Nocturne at Bethesda

#

CHAPTER 6

Flowers of Sacrifice

September 1, 1963

Those days in May, dragging on slowly and agonizingly for Desiree, eventually faded into a week. Weeks finally passed into June. Summer arrived in Philadelphia, hot and sweltering and carried on through the dog days of July and August. By September, there were obvious signs that Desiree had survived a threatening emotional and physical breakdown. Intensive care, however, and therapy, sometimes bathing two and three times a day, did not wash the filth from her body. It did not dissolve the guilt she felt from Mal blasting his body half in two.

Two years had passed since Mal and Grace had taken her in, but she still couldn't separate Uncle Mal's suicide from the massacre. New Years' came, her twentieth birthday passed, and by year's end Desiree still carried the burden of abandonment. Perhaps, she reasoned, because she hadn't been in her heart totally and convincingly committed to non-violence.

The workshops had prepared her for passive resistance but hate still raged in her spirit. She could not bring herself to even say that she forgave her oppressor, forget about loving him. She recalled, watching through fingers covering her face that maybe the fire in her eyes roaring at the low-life bastard's red neck made him so viciously mean. Then Paul's body hurdling down upon her and having fallen in shameful agony in the heat of that noble moment caused her to mourn Uncle Mal's death. The migraines persisted, some days worse than others. Doctors, clinics, faith healers at prayer meetings in a host of churches could not alleviate her debilitating condition.

At the Pentecostal House one Friday night, listening to pleading voices powerful enough to resurrect Lazarus from the dead, Desiree's father, Jim Pierson suddenly stood and began confessing to a life riddled with sin. He was a stocky and bald man of average height with muscular shoulders that looked like hams extending to his elbows. Desiree's mother, Rebecca Pierson, an angular woman of forty-five and a school teacher, was a fundamentalist. She wept unabashedly while pleading guilty to the maliciousness of silently seeking revenge on her daughter's perpetrators. Desiree, young, and naive, had been left all alone to fare for herself, Rebecca cried out to the ravaging wilderness in her mind. Who else, other than the handful of brave innocents like Desiree among the millions now better off, would have even attempted such a feat? God have mercy on her only child.

After pleading with her daughter to testify, to say all of whatever was on her mind at that very moment, Desiree spoke in an angry, clear monotone. "I am not my own problem." She had already rejected the Jesus bag—a suggestion that simply surrendering herself to Christ—become a born-again Christian would relieve her condition. Again she repeated. Her guilty stain was not herself; it was Tobacco Road America. A close friend of her mother's suggested that Desiree might be going mad. Rebecca's angry reply severed their friendship.

Since Desiree's tenth birthday, her mother admitted, she had always pushed, not allowing her daughter time for unstructured leisure, or the ease of making mistakes and learning from them. Not badgering, but by using a kind of steady manipulation, she had made Desiree an anxious, quick-witted child, and a hard loser. Always at the sweaty tip with one last surge of energy to be the best. Her mother's abrupt change to extremely pampering her, unsettled Desiree. Complaining didn't help.

On the Monday morning after the Friday of Desiree's twentieth birthday, her father gave himself to Christ. Jimmy-the-Brick they called him, a former prize-fighter, sent word to the South Philly mobster's boss at Seventh and Snyder. His time had come to close the lounge, get out of the business. When the mobsters arrived, Jimmy's piece and its clip lay on the bar with the week's payment to the bank. Though surprised, they didn't beat him and demanded nothing. Desiree never talked with her father about his livelihood, though she knew he worked for the South Philadelphia Syndicate. She wasn't aware of its running gun battles with Black Brothers Inc. The organized group of young gangsters were determined to run the young Mafioso Turks out of their community, and cash in on the horde of extorted money.

Despite her complaints, Desiree's parents continued smothering her with love. Her nightmares and crying spells increased after the assassination of President John F. Kennedy. Desiree believed she had earned a special kind of friendship with him and his brother, even though she hadn't known them personally. He and Attorney General Bobby, Desiree reckoned, saved the Freedom Riders from death by the Ku-Klux-Klan. God, you really got to help the Riders, and poor Mrs. Kennedy, she mourned. The President lost his life for saving ours.

In less excruciating circumstances the middle-class home, some distance up Germantown Avenue hill from the hard streets of North Philly, would have been adequate for wellness. Desiree's Mom remodeled the bedroom studio with glossy white and bright shiny shades of yellows. She bought a new spinet even though the old one hadn't been used much. After her mother's persistent beseeching to paint, Desiree began sketching her streams of consciousness. It was a drastic change of pattern compared to earlier works in her portfolio. Her mother cried at the fine pencil drawing of a black child, alone in a dirty whistle-stop restaurant, eating a ridiculously oversized hamburger. Grease dripped all over his clothes. Sliced raw onion rings piled high on the plate drew water from the child's eyes. Desiree doubted, from her mother's reaction to her sketches, that she understood her suffering. Rebeca indeed wrestled with a painful sense of guilt over not having paid adequate attention to her only child's emotional sensitivity.

Eventually, as Rebecca combed and brushed her hair Desiree began feeling an unfamiliar tenderness in her Mom's hands. She heard the subtle mumbling; begging Jesus' intervention to help recapture the warmth of innocence her daughter had lost. Desiree's mother plaited her hair in long, thick, and tight pigtails to enhance growth after it had been cut to treat wounds in her scalp. As much as she grieved the loss of her daughter's teen years, Rebecca only complained to Desiree that she had lost her toothpaste smile.

Desiree and her father often talked after he had become a born-again Christian. She learned that she had come to her parents' late. Brick had worked his way back to Philadelphia from the prize-fighters' last-chance dumping grounds in Toledo, Ohio. He read simple biblical phrases and told her about some ugly aspect of his former self to explain its meaning. Desiree suspected he was slyly exonerating himself from whatever about his past that was wicked, while the two of them spent long hours in physical therapy or in doctors' offices. The challenge of extracting fact from his hefty imagination often amused her. Even though she seldom smiled, quips like, "don't play the numbers on Sunday," did grant her the first opportunity she'd ever had to ask him little questions. His answers began opening her heart to him, which triggered conversations about the shotgun blast that tore out Mal's heart. So vividly did she explain the frightening sound, like dynamite blowing out a mountain of mud. Her wondering heart in beseeching her father to allay that fear, further diminished the barrier of emptiness between them—a gap of refusal to admit they really hadn't known each other.

One day, Jimmy told her they should drop The Brick, for he had outgrown that signature. He seized the opportunity to tell Desiree sensitive things imperative for a black man to plant in his daughter's psyche to encourage compassionate reasoning for the plight of black men in America. A little late, he admitted, and perhaps he had done little as an example. For certain though, now she understood why Mal couldn't live with himself any longer. Not because he was an old world-weary fool; Mal had spoken for an age of Negro men fresh off the battlefield. These warriors knew the viciousness of redneck hatred, of which she'd had her first brutal encounter.

Desiree, golden and magic like a spiritual the old folks sang for endurance, had found shelter in his home. By condemning him with her eyes, she placed a burden on his soul, and unknowingly cursed what little dignity he could rightly claim. She need not grieve anymore. His suicide, though unfortunate, was death to a way of life.

Desiree felt sad and humble. The dense band of migraine around her head slackened, even though the reference to a spiritual meant little.

"Did Billie Holiday sing them?"

"Well, I don't rightly know, except maybe when she was a little girl in Baltimore," her father said.

Desiree asked him to sing one, but he could not recall any. Desiree recognized the humorless smile and watched him rub his balding head. She wouldn't embarrass him.

Desiree had been the youngest of three Temple University's exceptionally bright sophomores excused from class to travel with the Freedom Riders. At Penn Central Station, she, another girl and a boy had boarded the train for Washington, DC. They vowed to stick together but were separated while attending passive resistance workshops.

Desiree returned to Temple while recovering. Several chums at school and church, all proud of Desiree's courage and the news worthiness, organized a tutoring team. They made her a scrapbook of the media's coverage of the Freedom Riders daily encounters. In '65, Desiree graduated. In those most critical hours of personal assessment, in cap and gown and promenading to Pomp and Circumstance, she tried measuring her worth in a confused mood. By then she had become a forgotten national heroine. All she could show of worthwhile teen achievements were the scrapbook keepsakes. It was a collage of Desiree and her comrades on time-worn cover pages of Newsweek and Time magazines, amid newspaper print about invading Dixie. She wondered sorrowfully about all of them, as if accepting the reality that they had been killed: Genevieve Hughes from Chevy Chase in Maryland, Edward Blankenheim from Tucson in Arizona, James McDonald from New York City, Mae Francis Moultrie from Sumter in South Carolina, Professor Walter Bergman and his wife Frances, James Peck, and so many others. A camera and rolls of undeveloped treasured film were destroyed in the firebombed bus. An old diary was her only keepsake. From her passages she had been encouraged, and indeed tried to write exactly what she felt about herself relative to her remembering those past ordeals.

Unfortunately, after re-opening those wounds grief, raw and primitive, began attacking Desiree at unpredictable times. She spent hours walking to no place in particular. Like the scatterbrained prize- fighters her father had talked about, hobbling from one gym to the next begging for one last fight to pay the rent, buy some groceries. Pain began settling in her hips, at times severely excruciating. Her blood pressure became erratic, peaking and falling. As her mother had suspected, wickedness had begun festering and would soon have a firm hold on Desiree's loins. That is why she had hurried Desiree to the Holiness Temple, hoping it could draw out the demon. Desiree's mother could not understand and prayed ceaselessly for release of her personal anger at Desiree for rejecting the Temple. In futile desperation, one last effort before she really didn't know what, Desiree sought a holistic physician.

The doctor's immediate prognosis, Desiree must first understand and then face the fact. She had been living in a twilight zone of conscience battering, all those years since the ordeal. She constantly relived those episodes, though perhaps not fully aware of the trauma of pain making it real. Then fighting back—adrenalin surging, hyperactive and sweating, until she would become exhausted and sink into a depression.

Desiree must stop identifying with agony. Freedom Riders had forced the Interstate Commerce Commission to outlawed segregation nationwide within interstate bus terminals. Was that not the objective? Stronger medication would mask the pain with an eighty percent likelihood that Desiree would become a writhing addict. Otherwise, the doctor could prescribe slow and lengthy chiropractic care. In time, Desiree would hopefully recover from the severe psychic and physical stress. She must concentrate daily to mend her will to live a useful life.

Concentration should eventually free her from the shadow of death—pain and unknown horror. The choice, her doctor explained, was Desiree's to make.

She disagreed with what seemed to be an eccentric prognosis, especially the veiled warning of death, which Desiree flat out rejected, and enrolled in the Kemetic Yoga Center. On a wintry Tuesday in November, Desiree nodded weakly to a warm greeting by Yogi Mehturt. The elderly, soft-spoken and rather tall chocolate complexioned man gingerly withdrew his hands from hers and massaged them as he welcomed her inside. Desiree tried to apologize for cold gloved hands, but stopped when he smiled and, with intense brown eyes full of caring, slowly shook his head.

"Please," he indicated with his hands, "Hang your things there, and put your shoes in the rack. If you like, put on a pair of sandals, or be comfortable in your stocking-feet. Would you care for herb tea, mineral water, or plain water?"

"I think nothing." Desiree tried to sound unguarded, as she acquiesced and followed him.

Beyond the vestibule, they entered a circular room, fifteen feet in diameter. Her favorite color, sky blue yoga mats covered one half of the area, the yoga and meditation space. Soft pastel-colored cushions were strewn about that area. A circle of eight soft lights extending on white chains from a mint green high ceiling, cast a peaceful ambiance over the entire space. Inhaling the calming fragrance of balm, lavender and myrtle eased Desiree's misgivings. The warm floor against her feet made them nice and toasty. Had she indeed been welcomed into a tranquil world?

"Might a spot of fenugreek tea relax your apprehension?"

"Oh, I didn't know it was obvious." Desiree forced a chuckle at his giggle. "Fenu?"

"Fen-u-greek. Its healing properties, not so much its taste, makes it a favorite especially in the winter time."

"Whatever you suggest."

"Then come. I'll pour and let's chat a spell."

They sat at a bamboo table in a snug alcove with a window, which overlooked the Chestnut Hill community. Desiree sipped the hot brew.

"Whew! No way without sugar"

"Will raw honey from a local beehive do? We don't use sugar."

"Sure, but how can this bitter tea possibly help me?"

"It alone probably won't be very beneficial, Desiree. Coupled though, with other nourishments it can control migraines, attack digestive and loss of appetite problems, ease muscle pains. Of course, others are just as helpful. Sip a little, then let's get started. I suggest we begin learning how to heal your spirit."

"How could you know anything about my spirit?"

"It is a good place to start, Desiree. Choose a pillow, let's relax." She sat crossed-legged on an orange-shaded pillow in front of him, sitting in the lotus position.

Yogi Mehturt placed his index finger to his lips and began talking in hushed tones. "Our phone conversation and your presence both speak loads. We start revitalizing the flow of healing energies to the hurting places in your anatomy."

"But sir." Desiree looked away from his gaze. "I am not comfortable with you so close and scrutinizing me."

"Scrutinizing is not my objective, healing is. Please stand erect, watch me, and do as I suggest."

Desiree stood erect and stiffly lifted her arms overhead in the mountain pose. "If I may," he asked and as she nodded, moved her arms to an exact vertical position.

"Can you lift them a little higher," Mehturt asked and stretched his several inches.

"Sure." She snickered and responded heartily.

"Well, okay," He responded. "They didn't move."

"What!"

"No. Stretch from your armpits to the finger tips."

"Oww, that hurts!

"Ease off, take a few deep breaths. Now, slowly stretch to your pain threshold again."

"I'm trying, but it's too..."

"Send energy there."

"How?"

"Breathe deeply into the pain." Seconds later a wary smile wiped the agony from her face.

"Lower your arms, relax and let them hang."

"They still hurt, but not as much."

"Good; gently raise them again."

Desiree observed, and breathing into the movement, she followed him.

"Lift your knee caps by tightening the thighs. Now, lift the abdominal muscles and your sternum. Very good. Tuck your tailbone under and contract the buttocks."

"Do what?"

"Tighten the buttocks and pull in your stomach muscles.

"That is not what you said a moment ago."

"Well, no, but it will get the same effect. Breathe deeply and relax."

"Is all of what I just did part of the Mountain pose?"

"Yes, let's do it once more."

Desiree followed, inhaling, and raising her arms overhead, stretching from her armpits to the little fingers. She exhaled heavily and though hurting and winded, stayed in the posture until Yogi Mehturt came out of it.

"When a person is severely attacked the brain sends shock to several organs in the body and shuts down. The shocked organs block your anatomy's energy and communication channels. Opening them is essential to healing. Now, completely relax. Let go."

"Standing here on my feet?"

"Why not!" Yogi Mehturt's amusing beam eased her tension. "Unless you are tired."

"Well, just a little woozy." Desiree wished she hadn't lied.

"I'll show you an alternate nostril breathing technique, and then we'll practice deeper relaxation."

Desiree put her thumb on the right nostril, inhaled and exhaled loudly through the left nostril. With two end fingers on the left nostril and breathing as forcefully through the right made her nose bleed. "Oh my," she exclaimed embarrassedly with blood on her hands.

Mehturt gave her a pack of tissues. "A nose bleed can be indicative of several things. Do you feel nauseous, or suffer from headaches and high blood pressure?"

"I take medicine for hypertension; have been for years."

"You are responding well to awaken kundalini, the life force in your body. We will heal you and lower the blood pressure."

"Do you mind? If I could just sit and listen, I am feeling a little hyper."

"Certainly, Desiree. This basic posturing is necessary to start the healing process. You will grasp the essentials as you become more aware."

The pains Desiree encountered in stretching beyond her comfortable limits in the passing weeks and months aggravated the soreness in her body and at times re-awakened the horrors of the Mother's Day massacre. Then, Yogi Mehturt would utter, his voice barely perceptible, "Loving a Supreme Being is impractical without loving yourself. Harder yet, is sincerely wanting to forgive. You and the Supreme Being are one; it resides within your soul. You will grasp the essential meaning of that as you became more aware and increase the spiritual quality within."

Desiree struggled on with anger and pain, but as she surrendered anger, pain subsided. Eventually a quieting calm began, while Desiree began meditating and learning the importance of leading a purposeful life. She taught yoga at the Germantown Friends Meeting, while amassing a reasonably profitable clientele of private students.

"Why was I born? Why is my name Desiree?" She sought a clearer understanding, spending hours alone pondering hers and the names of women in her family lineage. The personal designation of Desiree, the last born, was the subject of desire, desire being the mainspring of action. Grandmother Lady had named Rebecca, Desiree's mother, for its biblical significance. Great Grandmother Isis named Grandmother Lady to continue the uplifting of their spiritual selves in overcoming the demeaning yoke on black womanhood in slavery. *Capture me, use and abuse my body in your many gristly sinful ways of rape, but you'll neither stifle my dignity nor control the I of me, my soul, my spirit.*

Yogi Mehturt placed a lotus flower on Desiree's forehead the day in April of 1968, a sniper's bullet cut the voice, but not the psychic energy of Reverend Martin Luther King, Jr. "Desiree?" He spoke hardly above a whisper, "Like the lotus rising out of chaos, Doctor King is our Savior of the Black race in America."

She tried to speak. Yogi raised his hand. She knew that it meant, listen closely. "You are entrusted with his discipline to represent a spiritual revitalization. Do not to discuss what has been unveiled until you are certain Desiree can live in harmony with that concept of herself. Be aware, you will suffer from bouts of confusion and insecurity. Secure a suitable mate. The path of spiritual growth is long as life and at times not easily traveled, especially alone."

She began gathering unto herself, what Yogi called, a mythology of Desiree. She sought to grasp its purpose by painting again, practicing the piano, and meditating on discipleship. Gazing into her spiritual eye one day, Desiree was drawn to a space with a blue-sky background and a huge lotus flower opening its petals. Half of one petal had shriveled. Yogi nodded and said that she should know it represented the growth of her soul-potential. Then he said the time had come for Desiree to rely on her instincts without assessment by Yogi.

While assuring him she would find her chosen way, Desiree's voice rang with command. Nothing short of immersing herself in the redemption of society's worst examples of itself would suffice—the outcasts, the underprivileged, the unlearned, and the uninvited. She demanded, and her parents reluctantly gave Desiree back to herself.

She had reached that decisive point in her life two years before she met Reverend Alan Duberry. His appearance made her acknowledge that she had been lonely, a young woman's loneliness, noticeable by her heart rising thumps against her breast.

He, a young minister returning from Egypt, was drawn to her. She, a yoga adept, and a portrait artist with an incredible portfolio, attended the University of Pennsylvania's School of Social Work. Why, she gathered from the perplexed look on his face, had he wondered about that?

#

CHAPTER 7

Desiree Meets Alan

October 14, 1971

Like a wonder, Reverend Alan Duberry came into Desiree Pierson's days and nights, saying all the right things, including his perception of the Reverend Martin Luther King Jr.'s Promised Land. "Perhaps Desiree could be so intrigued?"

Desiree chose not to answer while having lunch in Old City Philadelphia's Middle East Restaurant, observing him with his fine self, digging her instead of the belly dancer. She had better slow him down and listen more carefully. He had a knack of prying and had told her way too much about himself in such a short time.

She had responded with the others at the Urban League's annual banquet to Reverend Duberry's graceful spread of his arms in quieting the crowd's thundering ovation. What a fine somebody, yes indeed, spreading charismatic charm like weaving magic over the formal affair at the Civic Center. No doubt in her mind, three or four Cleopatras desperate for passage to America, had chased him right up to the Egyptian airport's boarding gate. A peculiar one indeed, hair long, dark brown and combed down to his shoulders, eyes gray and mischievous.

Desiree listened, enchanted, and marveled, at how he so adroitly held the attention of the league's tuxedo and mink-stole-attired donors. While they had snacked on chocolate ice cream and coffee, after dining on two-hundred-dollar stuffed chicken dinners, his subtle and not so subtle criticism had made several persons more than uncomfortable. For certain, no one had been bored during the fully charged hour. When he banged his fist on the podium demanding strict attention, Desiree had thought, *my oh my.*

"All that we achieved from the social revolution of the sixties means naught unless it evoked a revival in your spirit. And we had better look further than these United States for that restoration of our true selves. For centuries, Mother Africa has been raped of all that is rich and precious by every nation in Europe, Asia, and by some of her own kind. Her black children are scattered to all four corners of the universe, defiled and denounced by every rogue-republic, while we who still call ourselves Negroes, feed and drink ourselves full of that foul denunciation."

Desiree could recall practically every word of Reverend Duberry's speech. He stopped, sipping water and waiting for the response, Desiree had presumed, noting the room suddenly almost as quiet as it would have been if empty.

"There is much more to us than a legacy of slavery. Whether one has the wherewithal to look is no excuse for one's neglect of knowing. If we could possibly open our hearts wide enough to behold our Motherland, servitude would become miniscule compared to the rich heritage that we would be better about reclaiming."

Sitting close enough to read his body language, Desiree had seen his eyes drifting over certain individuals, while he rubbed his right hand over his lips.

"Every race and ethnic group that has come to these shores from distant places brought with it a literary expression relative to its history. Every one of them had been ravaged in one respect or another by conquering armies, famine, internal strife, and disease. Yet, every one of them has added to the American anthology a particular legacy of before and after the European Renaissance. Historians have not been dedicated to the truth about us. The voices of our ancestral scholars have been silenced far too long. A draft of a legacy based on an African American Humanities, from which would spring an enduring revolution of self-respect and intelligence is overdue. We must gather those lost scripts of early Africa, place them in American annals. Consciousness of one's true self feeds on one's individual intellect. If we are sincere about helping more than a handful of our promising, attractive students who happen to fit a certain mold, we must invest in an African Institution of History. And I don't mean some jive-ass classroom in some abandoned water-front box factory."

Uh-oh, Desiree had thought. Up jumped his ugly side. She wondered why he had thought it necessary and made a mental note to ask him if she would ever get the nerve to let him hear her repeat it.

"Look backwards to 1591 to the Moors invasion of Ghana, Mali, and Songhai," the Reverend continued. "If we looked no further, wondering about it would dispel the ugly stigma we have worn since slavery. But don't stop there. Ponder the edicts in 4 AD and 6 AD of Roman Emperors Theodosius and Justinian. After they marveled at the wisdom and sacredness of the Kemites, those ancient Black Egyptians' relationship with an Almighty God by some other name, they revised the part of it that fit their needs and claimed it as the Romans' very own. For authenticity, they named it Christianity. Emperor Justinian converted the Egyptians with bloodied swords and trampling horses. Then he offered them Bibles of their revised religion, which they accepted, or fled for their lives to the interior of Africa. Some present-day historians have tried to claim the Egyptian part of Africa was not originally black, or that Egypt is not a part of Africa. In the long haul, truth will win over deception anyway. So we need not argue either point."

Desiree had begun applauding. Mostly the younger folk, black and white, joined her. Some stood, but Reverend Duberry waved them to their seats.

"If truth will eventually win, why am I railing on what I gather, many of you already know? Why am I wasting time, raving about an all but lost history? For the sake of our neglected spirituality, for our rightful place in the annals of civilization's structure, for admiration and honor, in place of loathing and pity."

"For those of you I haven't inspired, if you must continuously dwell on the horrors of slavery, for the sake of your sanity study the resilience of a people who endured. Become stronger, stop the self-loathing."

Stepping away from the podium, his wandering gaze stopped at Desiree. Desiree's heart had been urging her to learn more about him. He could be a glory hog. A pampered mama's boy with a fresh bag of tricks, loaded with philosophical rhetoric and looking for a warm bed, a cozy nest lined with gold nuggets. Though she wouldn't be that, neither would she let him get away.

There in the Middle East Restaurant sipping her coffee, she asked him, "Has there been much reaction to your speech?"

"Nothing much other than a decent check for services rendered. Say, what's good on the menu, and what should I avoid?"

"Just follow me. Today, I'll have something special. Let's see. Grape leaves, some falafel, and two slices of spinach pie."

Alan ordered a small hummus, a garden salad, six grape leaves, and a glass of water without ice.

"Some of it did sound too revolutionary for the League." Desiree hoped the Reverend would not ask her to explain.

His response was that if our music, art, and literature were viewed as expressions of fine arts, rather than popular stuff not worthy of religion, they would enhance our spirituality, make religion a more meaningful practice.

"You, an ordained minister, have problems with the way Colored folks do religion?"

The Reverend slowly fixed his gaze on the wall portrait of a snorting bull charging a panicking crowd. "Liking or not liking it is not germane to the problem. If we expect the reward Doctor King promised in that memorable speech, we must make our religion a greater attraction. Not enough leaders are helping their followers become worthy of that compensation."

"Hunh?" A bemused smile curved Desiree's lips. "How could you possibly know that?"

"Do you know of any groups or individuals touting Doctor King's banner except on his birthday? I sincerely believe it will require a spiritual rebirth. I know what is required. But I am not ready for the monumental challenge of helping others prepare themselves."

"How can you qualify if you're not ready?"

"I do not have a following, and I need a venue. Rather than brag about myself, or complain about my needs, I'd like to tell you a story about a little seven-year-old boy always accused of idle day-dreaming and inflating his imagination. You decide if I am qualified."

"Your motive is obvious, but I'd rather you didn't burden me with the responsibility of judging your fitness for what sounds like a life's obligation."

"Truth is, I have never bounced this off anyone. I only ask that you hear me out. Okay?"

"Like I am not really a captive audience." Desiree drew robust laughter from both of them. "What are my choices?"

"I owe you one. Thanks. This lad's mind would have been severely crippled, had it not been for an insightful, elderly woman. Mrs. Gyce, God bless her sweet heart, was the only person, who understood those alarming expressions that often burst from him of a time and a life before his. She told his parents, after hearing him say things beyond the scope of his imagination, that he was destined for a future impossible for any of them to presently understand. She called him, a gift to black American, but also a very sensitive boy who needed physical and emotional protection. Like a vacuum, she sucked him under her invisible wings. Not a mystic, Mrs. Gyce was a small, framed person with a dark chocolate complexion, and deeply spiritual. In that town, the black church was the center of its black community. Mrs. Gyce, a well-respected church elder, was the lad's Sunday school teacher, and fortunately his mother's good friend.

"This Mrs. Gyce protected his imagination?"

"No, she protected him from persecution, and cautioned him to discuss those thoughts that would suddenly rise up in his consciousness only with her or his mother."

"Reverend, are you implying what I think you are?"

"Reincarnation? Maybe, but to even whisper that word in small town Hastings, North Carolina would be worse than standing in an electrical rain storm cursing God. Mrs. Gyce knew the boy overheard her whisper it to his mother. And with a fiendish look in her eyes, she scared the lad to silence. 'Now that you heard it, never let that word escape your lips.' Needless to say, she piqued his curiosity."

"This is interesting enough, and apparently all about you. But hearing more about things that shaped your personality, made me really wonder. What do you sincerely think about Black folks practicing religion?" Desiree said.

"My feelings are mixed. If you can stay a while longer, my reasons will become obvious."

"Lunch was good, both our coffees are probably cold," Desiree giggled.

"Well," he said, rather sheepishly, and taking a sip. "Ooh!" He crinkled his face into a horribly amusing mask. "Ain't nothing more bitter than cold black coffee. Waiter, two fresh cups, please?"

"Now, Desiree; my what a pretty name. Can you possibly image the turmoil inside this lad? Bowing to Pharaohs, or on the Nile guiding feluccas into the wind, or an adult talking in a foreign language, the boy in the here and now can't identify?"

"No, I really can't" Desiree spoke hastily, annoyed by the sudden remembrance of her own bout with destiny. She felt perspiration on her forehead. Embarrassed that it might be obvious, she said, "It seems a mite warm. Maybe there was a sprinkling of too much white pepper. It's hard to taste, you know."

"May I?" The Reverend stretched across the table and gently dabbed her forehead, a soothing expression on his face.

With him too close for comfort, Desiree leaned back in her chair. "How did his mother and father react to their extraordinary son?"

"His mother shouldered the blame for birthing a weird child until he had grown out of it. She called it a blessing. His father would shake his head, and mumble, 'I'm laying odds, one hundred to one, there ain't five people in the whole wide world with a mind like our son's.' Then, his demand ended the discussions."

They both laughed heartily. Desiree noticed the Reverend leaning in his chair, his shoulders rounded a bit, and a spark of some indefinable emotion in his eyes.

"The boy spends a lot of time alone in a tree where he knows no one will find him." The Reverend spread his hands on the table, palms facing each other, working his fingers, individualizing the story. "In there he thinks deeply on Mrs. Gyce's or his mother's counseling on some situation that has taxed his mind."

"One Sunday after church," Reverend Duberry reiterated, "a song the choir had sung rings in the boy's ears, while he is in his sacred place. *Hush, hush, somebody's calling my name.* Then, coming from the slave graveyard, he hears a man's voice he does not recognize singing it. It makes the lad edgy, but he is getting use to this strange activity and does not panic. The sensation soon passes, only to return a month later. Again, after church, the boy hears the choir harmonizing. *Go down Moses, way down in Egypt land.* It too, rings in his ears. But the man's voice is overriding it. He appears to be arguing with the sky about the song's meaning."

"Arguing with the sky, Reverend?" Desiree chuckled.

"It surely enough seems like that to the lad, who is, quite frankly, glued by fright to his high perch. Then, the voice demands he come to the slave cemetery. The youngster is willing enough to take on the challenge, but ten feet or so from the rusting iron gate, fear overwhelms him. Straight away to Mrs. Gyce, he runs. She marches him right back to the cemetery and explains what is going on."

"The voices attached to the music are spirits inside him in the here and now, and from an earlier time, too. He is a very sensitive person, she emphasizes, born with a gift that if not used to free oppressed people, he will lose it. Then she speaks in a slow, grumbly voice, totally unlike the one that never failed to warm his heart. 'There is a blessing in all of this for you. Search for its meaning. Don't matter how long it might take. Son, can't be no worse hell than this one here on earth burning us alive.' Now Desiree, I hope my answer to your question on Black folk doing religion is acceptable. It is a pacifier; not enough substance in it dealing with racism to like or dislike."

Desiree smiled a thank you, though not a happy one. "I'll tell you my story one day, someday, probably soon."

The Reverend heard a discomforting expression in her voice. "I'd be honored if you'd call me Alan, or Du, if you like."

"I like Alan, your first name." She reminded herself to respond cautiously to his potent approach. "Alan Duberry from Hastings. Where in North Carolina is it?"

"In the low hills of the Great Smokies, not far from the North Carolina and Tennessee border. A small town with a gigantic personality, between Asheville, and Madison."

"Is it your personality that makes it so special?"

"It is a microcosm of all that is America. That makes it the ideal place for what I want to do with my life."

"Which is what, if I might ask."

"Continue Doctor King's work. Four simple words that describe a monumental challenge."

"Oh! Really?" startled Desiree responded, her eyes gleaming. "Weren't you a bit too young, to have been part of the decision-making apparatus in the Southern Christian Leadership Council?"

"I have thoroughly studied Doctor King, his speeches, and writings of what others have said about him. His responses to his adversaries. I was teaching school on the day he was assassinated," the Reverend replied.

"I, too vividly recall the day."

"What were you doing, if you don't mind me asking?

"Making a major decision." Desiree leaned away from the table; her eyes transfixed on an image in mind. "Finishing my last yoga session, and…" She bowed her head and looked deeply into the Reverend's eyes. "What happened next is personal. So tell me, what qualifies you to think you can fit into Doctor King's shoes?"

"I didn't say or imply that I was his equal. I am though, ready to hoist his banner, except as I said before. I need a place and people really serious about overcoming the crippling effects of racism."

"Like Doctor King, you are a minister, so why don't you talk religion?"

"I am interested in a heaven on earth, not in the sweet by and by. We don't have a clue to what happens after death. Spirituality is the path I have chosen to travel for specific reasons. I have a plan that I believe will attract followers, kill oppression, and offer a good life. Might you consider joining?"

"Uh-uh, not on blind trust. I, too, know a thing or two about trying to build faith on something that won't be revealed until death." Desiree had definitely made Alan aware that she had encountered something undesirable having to do with religion.

"It is impossible for us to imagine how badly we have been emotionally twisted by brain washing techniques that still bind too many of us in a slave mentality. If I were a cusser, a few choice words could more easily explain it."

"'Tis good that you aren't."

"No need to fret, Ms. Pierson. So, you are well-versed in the fine art of yoga?"

"Yoga is my lifestyle. I live and teach it."

"Uh-huh, then you are a spiritual person, yes?"

"Of course. I know your plans are tentative, but can you give me a sketch on how you intend to attract initiates?"

"I'll do better than a sketch. First, I will tackle institutionalized oppression—the invisible and overt barriers—and brain-washing techniques racists use on us. Much of it is beneath the depths of decent conversation. Are you sure you've a mind to listen?"

"I will rely on your ability to express it decently, but not if you're going to sit ten miles aloof." She giggled. "And don't call me Miss Pierson."

"Thank you, Desiree," he said, overtly expressing joy. "I must step back several hundred years in slave history, but only as a prefix to accurately show that I am aware of the size of my challenge, okay?"

"Okay, Alan, but don't preach."

"I really hadn't planned to, me fine lady."

"Oh, shut up." She snickered.

"Yes'm. I don't know how much of this you already know. So, don't let me bore you."

"I won't go to sleep, promise."

"Okay. This oppression was created and fed by laws, and customs that support white superiority—feeding the egos of the chosen, and black inferiority—crippling the minds of the oppressed."

"On every July 4th, we celebrate the birth of that oppression, and reaffirm its existence. On that day in 1776, all of North America was a slave empire. America commemorated the anniversary of its right to become a nation, and just as importantly, its freedom to escalate the slave-building empire."

"You sir," Desiree exclaimed, "Have got yourself quite a challenge."

"True, but I can't do it alone. Set the wheels in motion, yes. Attract worthy support, hopefully. Are you familiar with the name, Willie Lynch?"

Desiree shook her head. "Should I be?"

"If you are concerned about the black family structural deterioration."

"I am, most definitely." Desiree stared at Alan contemplatedly. "Does it have anything to do with Lynchburg, Virginia?"

"Practically everything. Lynch was a slaver from the West Indies who came to Virginia back in the 1600s and taught his making-a-slave philosophy to Virginians. He set the psychological blueprint for the perpetuation of slavery into action, Desiree. That defies imagination."

"Don't preempt me." Desiree noticed a growling content creeping in Alan's voice as he spoke more hurriedly.

"Okay. Try visualizing each leg of a slave tied to different horses, facing opposite directions. Then see him on fire and forced other slaves to watch spooked horses pull him apart."

"Oh, My God, no." Desiree placed her palms over closed eyes, trying to block out the image.

"It is damned brutal stuff." Alan stopped, having talked more gruffly than intended, and sipped water. "That is only a taste of his inhumane concepts, which gave slave-owners peace of mind for fifty or sixty years, until its brutality turned on itself. As ironclad as Lynch boasted it was, he was not aware that brutality breeds brutality. In July, 1831 Nat Turner, a slave in Southampton, VA, turned Lynch-bolstered white superiority into mass hysteria."

"I know the Nat Turner story."

"Yeah, it's fairly well-known. Did you know that when he was three, Turner could recall events that happened before he was born, according to his grandmother?"

"I hadn't heard that." Desiree said.

"Well, in August 1831, fifty slaves were executed for the gruesome murders of 55 whites. Turner got away, but he surrendered two months later. Doctors chopped his body into pieces and distributed his parts to the community." Alan drew in a long breath, and let it out slowly, shaking his head in disbelief. "Imagine, if you can, the rationale behind cooking his flesh into grease to make soap, and giving his bones away for trophies?"

"Using his soap to clean their bodies?" Desiree shuddered. "That smacks of a seriously demented mentality."

"Maybe madness had become a contagious disease." Alan rolled his eyes crazily at the ceiling. "Or Turner's spirituality and sense of rebirth encouraged him to make them see themselves wallowing in their uncivilized brutality. But no one involved, including historians and current writers ever considered Lynch's make a slave philosophy the monster that drove Turner to madness."

"They chopped and boiled Turner's remains down to nothing, trying to figure out why he was smarter than they, and what went wrong that drove him mad."

Desiree laughed heartily at the ludicrousness of it all. "Alan, I understand your purpose. As my guru, Yogi Mehturt, taught, what God instills can't be destroyed."

"Thank you," Alan exclaimed. "tell me, his name again? Your guru."

"Mehturt, why?

Egyptian?"

"Yes. Why is his name important?"

"Not his name so much as his race," Alan exclaimed. Lordy Lord, Lord, Lord. In the sweet by and by. How much more fortunate can a poor guy get. Wow!"

"Any time, now," Desiree demanded impatiently, "you can stop the monkey shines, and answer my question."

"I've stopped, Desiree. Ancient Egypt philosophy is written in hieroglyphics on the interior and exterior walls of those pyramids. Millions stare without a clue to its meaning, but I know that quite a bit of it is about our innate spirituality."

"Egypt influenced your philosophy of black America?"

"Yes. I am building on something like the Kabala, to eliminate systemic oppression."

"Oh, really? Why?"

"You are aware?"

"Only of the term and a little of its meaning."

"No such law can be written to outlaw racism, which in many instances, is invisible. There is though, a way, I believe, to render it ineffective. The more oppressed persons I can attract, and raise their levels of spirituality, the greater will be the force to eliminate it.

"But aren't you afraid? No one ever need question Doctor King's bravery. He was a stalwart giant of a man, but I did see him back away. Good that he did. Saved his life, at least for a while."

"You?" Alan stared in awe at Desiree. "You were a …"

"Freedom Rider, the Mothers' Day Massacre in Anniston, Alabama."

"Desiree! You are a celebrity."

"Only for a quick minute in history. It's an involved story, Alan." The despairing glint in her eyes disturbed him.

"Maybe we'll get an opportunity," Desiree said, "to share it, some other time. About you though. I admire your drive, but your project is as alien as Russia's Kremlin to Black Americans."

They both laughed heartily.

"I am not a fortune-teller. You dear friend, are taking an awful chance on getting tarred and feathered, the modern way. American Christians, especially Born Agains and Evangelicals, the Nation of Islam?"

Alan sighed woefully. "What is the modern way, Ms. Pierson? When, not if, my project catches on, it will become a way of life. I am not afraid, though I accept your concern in the spirit that it is given." He pivoted his half-filled glass of water back and forth between his palms and cocked his head right-wise. "Ya know, Ms. Pierson…"

"I'd really like to be Desiree again." The radiance in her smile, and allure in her eyes coaxed him. "Would you?"

"My pleasure." Though harkened, he was more than a little disturbed by the warning. "If Mrs. Rosa Parks, or Doctor King had yielded to adverse pressure, we wouldn't be together here having dinner and discussing it."

"I am a witness, Reverend…"

"I'd rather be Alan to you, if I could."

"Yep." Desiree's eyes widened with a wink that melted the Reverend right down into his shoes. "I didn't mean to ice down your motivation. I just had to sort of, well I guess just to encourage you to think a little deeper. I know a little about local community mores."

"I appreciate your straightforwardness."

"Well, please don't read anything not said into this, Alan, "but I am concerned. Now, precisely, how will you attract?"

"OK. We presently exist in a state of not exactly physical terror, but a heightened state of fear. Ku Klux Klan, police brutality, and a failure to interlock as one united front. Our children grow up and fight the same systemic oppression. Our spirituality lays dormant. I must awaken it."

"It sounds worth all the effort you can put into it." Desiree chuckled at a devilish smile dancing in Alan's eyes, and his awkward attempt to express budding affection.

"Any man worth his salt must decide for himself the requirements for his passage into manhood. School, the university and seminary taught me, indoctrinated me, brainwashed me. Whatever the case may be, none of it prepared me for what I think I must do. I didn't realize it until I went to Egypt. There I found what I needed, which raised my level of self-competence. It is not easy to explain, at the end of lunch in a room full of prying ears. But for sure, Desiree, I speak as the man, and do my level best to act as the man I earnestly hope I exemplify."

Desiree stared at him, mesmerized, her mind soaring in her own memories. The determination-laced sensuality in his voice coming to a sudden halt interrupted her reverie. She sighed.

"My heart cries out to tell you more, Desiree, but I'm afraid I'll scare you away. We know so very little about each other."

"I have been to hell for the cause of freedom, right up to the edge of wits end. So you really needn't be so concerned about startling me."

Alan heard the sting in her voice and changed the course of their conversation. "I doubt Doctor King knew the depth of his pleading to Black America."

"Precisely what do you mean?" Desiree asked.

Alan blew a long, audible breath, and sat erect. "Do you remember him saying, we've got some dark days ahead? I believe he knew that passive resistance, the methods of appealing to men and women of good conscience in a morally sick society had worn thin. But he did not indicate that he was aware of the scourge laid upon the Old Race of ancient Egyptians by shutting down their Mystery System and using it for Christianity. It's hard for me to believe he didn't realize it is a fundamental reason for racism. Yet, the only hint of an indication he gave is in that famous line, *I've been to the mountain top.* What did he see? Who really knows? He simply said, *'I've seen the Promised Land.'* I think that was either empty rhetoric or a cover for what he suddenly chose not to reveal. I suspect he knew the moral conscience of America would have to be convinced it had been baited and deceived into a demoralizing race consciousness by the Roman Emperors. They were the shapers of Christianity. His *Letter from Birmingham City Jail* indicates as much. But I don't believe he knew how because I have not read, neither has anyone told me he knew the facts that would answer the question, why."

"Do you mean to overcome the scourge?"

"Yes. The American black social stratum revolves around that core of inferiority. A basic problem is the refusal to acknowledge the truth of our condition. We're sick, in a nation getting sicker in its efforts to devise more ways to spoon-feed a handful of rewards to its good Negroes. Except that we have damned the word *Negro,* deleted it and every one of its corrupting synonyms from our vocabulary, won't you agree?"

Desiree's eyes, perspicacious and wet, like a woman having lifted a veil, bathed him. Yes, he had strummed an emotional cord.

"I cannot understand how you, a minister slamming…"

"Not Christianity, Desiree. The shapers of it. Priests in the temples of the Old Race in Kemet were handed down the treasurers of bringing civilization, garmented in salvation, to the world. Christianity is the brainchild of the Old Race's Mystery System. That is where Reverend King would have had to go to reclaim our spirituality."

"Exactly what is there about how we got from there to here that makes it so negative?" Desiree asked, noticing the sudden down casting of his eyes.

"I will tell you, probably later."

"Why?" Desiree uttered a laugh bubbling in ridicule.

"My perception of it is raw. No one need ever wonder about the level of my indignation."

"Why don't you let me decide that?"

"I am afraid to chance it." Alan reached across the table for her hands, but drew back, suddenly aware that she might read his move as manipulation. He sighed. "But sooner rather than later we must deal with it, if we are to ever understand and stop underestimating the level of devastation, the graveness of our inferiority. Desiree, if you still insist, I only ask, if a need arises to forgive me, please be as candid as you expect me to be sharing this."

"Well," Desiree said, "I'm waiting."

Silence engulfed them. Alan doodled on the table with a fork. An angry pout forced the ends of his lips downward. Desiree waited; a strong wave of apprehension coursed through her. Then Alan unleashed the flood.

"The dog yanked black womanhood by her hair and pulled her dress up around her shoulders. Then he lashed her buttocks with his belt, thrust his penis in her uterus or rectum. At the height of his filthy orgasm, he screamed demands that she cry out in ecstasy to his Christian God. He'd struck the source, all but completely severing divine motherhood. Separate the divine in womanhood from any race or indigenous people, and that race is doomed to death. Fortunately, the dog didn't understand spirituality. His aim was to inflict torture so viciously on the physicality of black womanhood that he could control the emotional, and in time render her men completely docile. He plunged America into chaos that worsened as time passed until Reverend King began raising lethargic America out of its age of barbarism."

Desiree stared at the anger blazing in his eyes. Her voice broke. "Oh, God." She began shaking at fearful images forming in her mind.

"Scholars, black and white have been trying to tell us these things in a nicer way, but we shun them."

"Stop it!" She sobbed, poising a trembling hand to strike him.

Riled at himself for having let deep-seated resentment tear control from a personal promise to use compassionate reasoning with this subject, Alan leaned across the table. The palm of Desiree's hand resounding off his face jolted him. An acute implosion ripped inside Alan. Yet, he tried comforting Desiree, aware of the maitre'd approaching them.

"If what I've said hurt you." Alan pleaded quietly, ignoring the demanding urge inside him to back off, way off, like shut up, stupid.

Desiree placed both hands over her eyes, her body engulfed in a tidal wave of misery.

"I heard every word the venomous brute uttered," a woman sipping water at the next table with a man, told the headwaiter.

Desiree, peering from behind hands wet from tear-stained eyes, cut a lethal glance at the woman so mean she spilled half the glass-full in her lap.

"If you might consider..." Alan helped Desiree from the chair. "I'll drive you home and take a cab to my place. I hope this is not goodbye," he said, leading her through the doorway.

Desiree pointed to a telephone mounted on the wall. "Call your cab. Now!"

#

CHAPTER 8

Conscience of a Benevolent Society

October 28, 1971

Obviously, Desiree reasoned, the Reverend had returned from Egypt more unsettled than he had been during the civil rights struggle. He had alienated her. For several days, she thought deeply about his gross resentment, and though his angry explanation was disgusting, she couldn't disagree. However, his temperament was that of an idealist, too impractical. He was an infuriated young black minister, and with good reason, but she could not go down that angry trail again.

The doorbell ringing broke Desiree's unsettled concentration at the piano. With deliberate slowness, she went to the intercom mounted at the door. "Yes?"

"Reverend Duberry, wishing desperately to speak with Ms. Pierson, however briefly if I may."

"For whatever possible reason?"

"Ah, ah, well…s'cuse me for stammering. There are several I suppose, era I know for certain. I'd probably fail though, asking a weather-beaten intercom to weigh the truthfulness in my heart with a bouquet of violets, rose of Sharon, and chrysanthemums."

"Why?"

"This squawk-box is devoid of feeling. It has never been challenged with caring."

"Have you?"

"Why, yes ma'am, and I accept the challenge. Besides, it has started to rain, a cold drizzle, Desiree. Ms. Pierson, please?"

The peculiar surge of affection Desiree felt frightened her again. She liked the Reverend, but wished she didn't. Though she couldn't reason why she didn't. She believed he harbored a mean streak. Well, she did too, especially against overt racism. The ministry was his forte, identifying sin. And he had, in its most vile form, though he had caused her public humiliation. And yes, he was driven to acquire the same two basic things for which all men worth their salt strive: love and a position on the first team.

"If influenza carries me on home to glory, dear lady, the temperature won't be the demon, era, I mean the culprit."

"You'll need more than a silky tongue and summer flowers to get in here."

"I'll just park myself right here on your stoop until the police arrest me for vagrancy, or some high potentate rides up in a chauffeured Rolls

Royce. I'll not compete with mere scrapings of the material world for your attention."

As casually as Desiree could, she said, "My attention, hah. You don't know doodle-lee squat about it." She would never admit how much his admiration swayed her.

"About squat I won't disagree. But do you think I have not heard your heartbeats shifting to sync with mine?"

Desiree said, "I think you are acting pretty darn silly."

"I can't be silent about what we both know is real, and a crowd is gathering."

Desiree ignored the protective sense that warned her. She really didn't have much of a reason to reject him. "Come on in." She energized a switch that released the lock and let him enter the building. She cracked open the door to her apartment. "It is open," she said in response to his knocking. "I can only spare a minute or so. Please, park your shoes at the door."

"Busy doing what, if I may ask?" The Reverend stepped inside, closed the door, and complied. He walked up a few steps from the door well to a large and busy room, where she stood in yoga attire, feeling uncomfortably warm at her ability to sense his thoughts.

"They are beautiful." Desiree took the flowers. "Thank you." She curtsied.

"This is home." She waved her hand, in a manner of guiding his attention to her space. A new spinet sat in a corner across the room with some rough sketches of musical compositions, which were obviously

Desiree's. Close by were her yoga mat, mediation cushions and an aromatic fountain, sitting on a small marble-top table. A partially portioned kitchen area, replete with walnut cabinets and a counter top, a refrigerator, wall oven and electric range occupied a distant corner. A five-piece mahogany dinette set with four place mats, embroidered in pastel colors, complemented her cooking and eating zone. Along the opposite wall were two closed doors, and an over-stuffed easy chair, a small couch, floor pillows and a lamp. Desiree led him into a smaller room where bits of art paraphernalia, unfinished work, and journals were strewn about the cozy space. Three floor-to-ceiling portraits mounted side by side on a vanilla wall demanded his attention.

"May I?" Before she could answer, he switched on ceiling track lights above them, which cast pathways of soft light.

"What a terrific expression of one's soul." He immediately felt a kinship with a portrait of Jesus extending his hands down to lift a stumbling woman in tattered clothes from scorching desert sands. A potent level of energy flowed from Jesus, through the woman, to him, and back to Jesus. Its symbolism, he remarked, was indicative of Desiree working at expressing release from her torment. He asked questions, but Desiree simply smiled, indicating she would not discuss her artwork, other than to tell him the name—*Mary Magdalene*. Of the three paintings, Alan cared the least for *Moses and the Sea*. It was a depiction of an old man with a long white beard carrying a scroll and begging miniaturized people of different sizes to hurry. Clearly, the rapidly closing split in an angry sea would swallow many in the unending line.

Desiree stared at Alan for a moment, realizing he was skillfully worming his way into the secret side of her. She would not resist, as his insightful commentaries began melting her not hostile, but a cautious resistance. Desiree explained how the angry sea illustration fit the Willie Lynch plantation mentality that he had described the other evening. He agreed that it captured less intelligent and unfortunate persons who were trapped in their misery. Though the portrait was Desiree's interpretation, he suggested that it could be perceived as insulting. He thought *Chaos*, a graphic depiction of a revolver's blast killing a score of young people, was a more fitting title for the third one. It adequately illustrated the violent force of fire hoses washing people into a sewer, at a housing project entrance overrun with frantic individuals trying to get inside. Desiree stared at it pensively until he cleared his throat.

"Please be gentle if I am wrong."

"About what?"

"Considering what you have already shared, might this be a way for you to heal emotional scars?"

She hesitated, measured his comment. "Some days more so than others."

"Well, ah, sometimes, a caring person can offer needed relief." He looked at the floor, avoiding Desiree's eyes. "If I can ever help you understand what might be confusing..." He turned from Desiree and stood by the door.

Desire, watching him from the top step, suddenly felt despairingly lonely. "That was meant to be a back-handed apology I suppose." Her voice, low and irritated.

He looked up at her. Desiree noted his gentle eyes full of pleading. She stepped down and leaned forward, her lips half-parted and quivering. Her breathing short, and unsteady. His long shirt-sleeved arms encircled her anxiously. Their lips met in one nervous moment of rapture. Desiree's slender body drawn up against his set his lips trembling. They kissed long, gradually releasing each other's pent-up longing. Then placing her hands on his chest and with misty eyes, Desiree pushed away against his reluctance and determination to hold her at least at arms' length. They stared dumbly at each other.

"Alan, I shouldn't have..."

"Desire and love are as big as the whole wide universe. We are but two twigs of sugar canes wanting to entwine for nourishment."

"No, Alan, this is all wrong."

The Reverend released her. "Sorry again. Maybe if I weren't so insistent. I shouldn't have intruded. Yoga people are of a special mind-set that demands a lot self-examination."

"It does require a strict discipline, if that's what you mean, for..."

"A discipline I must learn as soon as I can. I meditate, but only to the extent of becoming the disciple of my chosen beliefs."

"Yoga is ritual as well as therapy for me," Desiree said, having regained control of her emotions. She would not fool herself by tempting love. "It helps me maintain my sanity." She wished he would explain his discipleship but decided against asking. A sadness clouded her brown eyes.

"Your being lost in thought begs an explanation, if I may, Desiree."

"I've something I must tell before this goes any further. I told you I was in Anniston, Alabama, remember?"

"The Mother's Day massacre, yes. You were a gallant freedom rider."

"Something you must know," Desiree said. "But I'll not be pitied."

"Pity, for such a noble deed? Please let me…"

"No!" She gruffly waved him off and opened the door, avoiding the question in his eyes. "I carry the scars, sir. I'm barren. Please go."

"Not for that reas… No, wait!"

Desiree almost caught Alan's nose in the door. He heard the deadbolt slip into place.

Bound up in her loneliness, the taste of Alan's kiss lingering on her lips, Desiree forced herself to admit that he had slipped beyond the boundaries of her inner guard. Alan would be the only male other than her father who'd ever know her condition.

For days after he had departed, Desiree quarreled with herself. She could not reign in her emotions. Two anxious weeks later, a letter arrived.

Dear Desiree,

I am not writing to sweet-talk, though you are heaven-sent. I will not indulge you in a lengthy explanation but permit me to say that until recently I had not one clue how to carry out my mission. Thanks for listening, sharing, and giving me insight. Now I have a plan, but I can't develop it or even consider putting it into practice alone. I believe you would be an asset to my pursuits and yes, I need you for far greater reasons than desirability.

Tehuti, the ancient Kemites' high priest, says for all things there is a reason, and for all that we do or propose to do there is a season, ebb and tide. Please do not despair, flowers of sacrifice bloom the lunar year. I am preaching on the second Sunday and would be so humbly honored if you'd attend.

Sincerely,

The Reverend Alan W. Duberry

"Whooo-weee!" Desiree's guttural exclamation ran to the end of her exhalation. Flowers of sacrifice bloom the lunar year? Corny, but masterful persuasion. Apparently, tact he had acquired. What could it possibly mean? Something to do with her? Probably, but he wouldn't dare put her in his sermon. He'd better not, though she wouldn't place him above speaking some code language meant only for him and her to understand.

Her mind raced on. No thanks, Desiree decided. Though she might change her mind, she wouldn't send him a reply. Desiree argued with herself, wrestling with indecisiveness, all the way to his church, and walked in on the service, late.

Eleven–twenty am on a cool mid-autumn Sunday, Assistant Pastor, Reverend Alan Duberry had already begun preaching to a small, but attentive group. When Desiree entered, all heads turned away from him and followed her as she followed an usher to a middle pew. Even he hesitated, waiting for her to sit. She was indeed elegant, dressed entirely in blue—a wide-brim powder blue hat, suede high heels, navy blue dress, and stockings. Someone cleared his throat, thus switching attention back to the minister.

"Despite everything accessible to teach us better, we still feed on an illusion thousands of years old. Regardless of all the opportunities available for questioning and knowing one's true existence, we accept as real, the myth of African Americans' distant past. We have been severed from our ancestors. Accept it or not, many are the ancient giants in the land of Egypt on the continent of Africa, the Kemites."

Reverend Duberry read. "*There were giants in the earth in those days, and also after that when the sons of God came in unto the daughters of men and they bear children to them, the same became mighty men, which were of old men of renown. (Genesis 6:9)*

"How sad it is at this late date, that we actually believe we are descendants of Cain. As such, our young spirits fall far too early from Cain's tree, being immature like green apples festering with maggots of wicked ignorance. Like insensitive fools, we lavish ourselves with soul food, soul music, soul dance, soul rap, soul this, soul that until the expression has become a watered-down buzz word. Truth is, wherever one might position that great crossing into the Promised Land in one's metaphorical geography, we don't have enough sustaining soul power to even get us across a shallow tributary of the River Jordan. Soul power is derived from the veneration of one's ancestors. If you understand, let me hear an amen."

After several seconds passed, "yas, yas," a male voice softly spoke.

"My, my," the Reverend said disgustingly. "And Jesus wept." He made a sound clearing his throat and continued. "It means little knowing grandma's body is in the hillside cemetery behind Half-Acre Methodist and her soul is in heaven. We must strive to understand what grandma's soul knew, and grandpa's too, when it departed from his body down there by the backwaters of Charleston, South Carolina. Guess what folks? That knowledge is actually in you. It must be awakened and sustained in trust. For our own greatness, we must first awaken their energy, and then search for evidence that will bear witness to our new-found knowledge. Listen to your hearts urging you to search among the annals of Sankore University, in the ancient city of Timbuktu. Follow the trails of pilgrimages the priests, professors, and scholars made across the Egyptian desert to Punt, the holy place. And when we become intelligent enough—grounded in faith established by knowing without a doubt—we will honor our ancestors magnitudes more, and fully grasp the inherent meaning of soul power."

"Though prayer grants confidence, it requires perseverance and keeping your mind on the objective. And Church, I promise you." Reverend Duberry accentuated his words by pointing his finger. "Prayer and endurance will result in earning the prize. Do not be so concerned about how, or how will you know it will nullify psychological bondage. How it will happen is a mystery. If it were known, evil forces would have found a means to block it. The wisest persons in the land cannot devise a means to block what is willed individually by my and your," he pointed to several persons, "individual acceptance of the end result. The result is that we will know and venerate our Egyptian-African ancestors who molded the world civilization. If anyone doubts they can do it with prayer and perseverance, I'll ask one question. I hope you will be truthful; you have only yourself to answer to. How many still honor Doctor Martin Luther King? Please, a show of hands?"

He scanned the congregation and is encouraged by at least a two-thirds response of about sixty persons. "Learning how and then venerating our ancestors will raise us emotionally above and beyond the atrocities of slavery. By venturing deep into the spiritual core of ourselves and meditating, which is a form of prayer, we awaken what is asleep deep within our consciousness."

"Go back in time to Ethiopia, Nubia, and Egypt. Move down through the ages, like the Nile flowing north, from the hills of Ethiopia to the Mediterranean Sea and beyond. Revere those magnificent priests of the Egyptian Mystery System, and scholars in Sankore University of Timbuktu, who studied in much the same way some of us do now. A restorative consciousness, which will result from this endeavor, will render it spiritually redemptive. Then we shall know once and for all time who we really are."

Desiree noted, as she had done at the Urban League banquet, he preached so thought-provokingly. His message was not easily interpreted, she reasoned was why she heard so few amens. The Reverend seemed to challenge a congregation that did not want to be challenged. Scattered amens were generally an indication, they rejected his sermon. Yet, the mellowness of his rhythmic-weaving intonation quickened her pulse and erased her fear of the unknown about him.

Reading from a list of names given him to acknowledge as visitors, he asked if anyone had been overlooked. Desiree stood, and after graciously accepting his greeting she readied herself to ease away quietly. His gazing held her spellbound. Watching her watch him, he marched by singing with the choir its last song before the benediction. Desiree caught herself yearning for an intimate spiritual closeness, but not like with a guru. Yes, the Reverend had penetrated her emotional barrier. She would not deny desiring him physically. Her smile opened into beaming admiration, while shaking his hand after service.

"You should consider taping your sermons." Desiree noted his sidelong glance of disbelief.

"For posterity's sake? Who'd buy them?"

"Your messages are quite like you, potent and so insightful. You defy the status quo with a vengeance, I do believe."

"I don't preach just to satisfy a Sunday's congregation, if that's what you mean." Amusement flickering in his gray eyes.

"I must confess." Desiree stepped back and suppressed a sigh. "I feel queasy standing so close to you. Well, maybe that's not the right word." She fanned her hand across her mouth, as if waving the word from it. "If I get to know you better..."

Reverend Duberry burst out laughing. "I promise not to bite, and I don't suck blood."

"Hoo-hoo," she sarcastically replied.

"Seriously Desiree, my sermon was about redemption from the psychological bondage of slavery. Living in that state of mind is a sin."

"A sin?"

"Yes, committed against one's self."

"I must say, you make redemption seem necessary."

"It is, but not easily acquired unless a person is dead serious about changing their lifestyle. And before you ask the question, my plan is working itself into a blueprint to eventually liberate millions locked in that bondage mindset. Say, can you stay a while longer?"

Desiree nodded. "Isn't that what you were offering, a way to earn redemption through prayer and faith?"

"Well, yeah, but by more tangible means. Like yoga and meditation. This idea, by the way, came from you. I recall two tangible examples of how redemption really works. One is Caribbean history, the Haitians whipping Napoleon Bonaparte. And I'd rather stay away from that one. The other is the evolution of American culture, which includes African Americans chopping away the falsehood of African's barbaric past. Like those acclaimed musicians spiritually reuniting with their ancestors."

Desiree's heart rate increased. She ached to hear more. "Why do flowers of sacrifice bloom the lunar year?"

Alan laughed heartily. "Okay, okay."

"Don't tease, tell me."

"Poetic metaphor, not mine originally but it keeps begging for a personal explanation. This isn't jive, Desiree. Flowers are nourishment for the soul. Sacrifices are offerings of atonement. Bloom means flourishing or coming of age. Lunar, having to do with the moon, one of the seven governors circling earth each month, the time between two full moons, twelve of them being the..."

"Lunar year," Desiree interrupted. An expression of skepticism swept across her face. "But your explanation doesn't capture the essence—the beauty of flowers changing each month."

"Okay, so you have some idea of where I am going with this. Jazz music is one of the best mediums that reunites us with our ancestors. We, those among us, who understand are caught up in that spiritual tidal swell. Are you an aspirant?"

Desiree laughed, though she really didn't know why. "Flowers, lunar moon, atonement; I'm wondering if this is all one big line of scratch, and you may be one big jive-turkey."

"Whew! Answer me and find out."

"Growing up with Jimmy (the Brick) Pierson, I didn't question much and believed little of what I did question."

"Jimmy the Brick?"

"My father, he ran a popular night club until he got saved and found his personal Jesus. Do you know of any jazz musicians practicing yoga? Some probably do, I suppose."

"Yes, Alice Coltrane, jazz harpist, for one. Horace Silver is another. Why wouldn't they? I've read yoga texts and worked at it some, but I haven't studied it as you have. Isn't it about achieving, what to the individual, seems unachievable by any other means except through meditation and a disciplined lifestyle?"

"Yes, but Alan, surely you are aware of the drug scourge associated with the grueling lifestyles of musicians, which has ruined so many beautiful people and careers. I don't want to see the crippling effects of that, and I don't care to be in that debasing environment."

"Neither do I. So let's not stereotype. Come with me this evening, judge for yourself."

"Whoa! You're rushing me. To where?" Desiree asked For what?"

"Jazz vespers at The Old Pine Street Church at six."

"Are you insisting?"

"Well, yes, if you put it that way."

"Maybe I can meet you there."

"Have I earned the courtesy of a call if you opt out?"

"I think so." She gave him an assuring smile.

"Better yet, how's about a stroll along East River Drive and dinner first?" Alan asked

"Dinner with Mom and Dad today. Suppose I stop by for you at, shall we say five thirty?"

"Forty-fifth and Spruce. I'll be waiting at the corner."

#

CHAPTER 9

Groovin' High Naturally

November 6, 1971

After her supper and right on time, Desiree drove up to the curb where Alan waited. He opened the door and getting in, sneaked a peep at her tantalizing legs. Desiree chuckled and drove away.

After driving along cobblestone streets in historic Philadelphia, she parked, and they entered the Old Pine Street Presbyterian Church sanctuary. "My, but this is an old building," she remarked.

"Venerable churches smell dank," Alan said, like the earth after a heavy rain, or like time-fragile books locked up in antique book cases."

He was coming on too strong. It annoyed Desiree. She would rather move a little slower, sample him cautiously, study him defending his convictions. "Alan, Reverend Duberry, it is a bit strange, at least to me, that you, a kind of a hard-nose black minister, likes jazz so much."

"Me, hard-nosed? Well, if that's how you see me, I probably am. Yes, I do love jazz and for good reason, which I will gladly explain. Where would you like to sit? "

"Oh." Desiree chuckled at his tact of masterful persuasion. "Wherever."

"Right down front for me, center section where I can see the musicians' hands, the expressions on their faces and hear their drones as they create. Jazz vespers speak to a form of worship at the rising of the evening star. It is part of African Americans' intellectual heritage and germane to our claim to rights in MLK's Promised Land. Most likely, the minister here and lay persons understand the fine arts as it pertains to evolution and spirituality. By tying the two—divine worship and jazz— spirituality grows. The two do not clash for those who really want to understand."

"Alan, are you off on one of your truth-seeking excursions again?"

"Not really."

While the musicians tuned-up, Alan explained how jazz pertained to evolution and spirituality. "Slavery did its best to rob us of our ancestral knowledge. It kind of like, went underground then reappeared as Jazz, and employs the symbols in the artist's ethnicity to convey impressions of the human soul. Individual expressions spring from a deep and mysterious necessity. Is that explanation worthy of your ear, Ms. Pierson?"

Desiree smiled acceptance. He certainly had his wits about him. Vespers began as she played with his name, slowly reciting it to herself repeatedly until she felt comfortable saying it. "Reverend Alan Duberry," she purred, suddenly realizing that he was deciphering every utterance. "I really don't know you well enough to be sitting so close and being mesmerized by a trio playing Miles Davis' *Blue In Green*."

"Blue is February's moon, the color of purification, of loving one's self, and forgiving past errors. Green is August's moon color, an approaching time for harvesting and appreciation, bursting colors of summer flowers. Green is Miles' choice of colors. "It is addictive." Alan chuckled. "Ah, the music I mean. You needn't hunt for a reason to be afraid of me."

They sat in silence and listened; Desiree watching him from the corner of her eye, Alan attempting several times to hold her hand. The session ended, Alan and Desiree applauded and smiled satisfaction to each other. The musicians excused themselves for a break. Alan closed his eyes momentarily and then looked at Desiree, his eyes full with contemplation.

"Flowers of sacrifice bloom the lunar year. Desiree, I'm asking you to help me."

"Help you do what?"

"Find a way to redeem lost souls from the psychological bondage of slavery."

"Uh-uh. God no!" Desiree shook her head. "I've been there, paid my dues, and for what? Once in a lifetime is enough, sorry." Then something clicked in Desiree's consciousness. She thought of Yogi Mehturt. *Tranquility would come as evolution's requirements of her were revealed, accepted, and fulfilled. Like Martin Luther King, Jr., Desiree symbolized the Golden Rule.* She had no reason to push Alan's words away. Listen to him, do not let the ego interfere.

"Why me?" she asked.

"You know the answer better than I."

"How could you possibly know that? I am not a mirror."

"No," Alan responded, "but I believe the degradation you endured has made you something special. That experience obviously changed you from something, probably from an average college student into a knowledgeable and fearless leader. We'll talk some more after the vespers, okay."

Desiree nodded approval and settled back in her seat. After an hour or so of good vibrations, the session ended. Desiree and Alan stood and joined the others in applauding. She sighed, murmuring satisfaction.

"Want some refreshments?"

"No, I don't think so. I want to hear your explanation."

"I know," he said quietly, holding open the sanctuary door for her, as they stepped out into the Old Pine Street night. "I believe your desire to love is buried under a rubble of protective disorder, but it is waiting. You have been identified for the cause of redemption."

Even while she listened, started the car, and drove off loaded with trepidation, Desiree loved the way he spoke, revealing the person she really liked. That uncompromising tone of his voice, the tender but stern expression on his face, the quiet depth in his eyes bespoke of an abundance of masculine appeal. "Very good, Reverend Duberry," she said. "Tell me more about myself."

"Okay, but I'd rather wait until you know more about me."

"What faster way is there for me to know you than by hearing what you see in me?"

Reverend Duberry heaved a sigh, a warning Desiree ignored.

"You were a heroine, Desiree, and then you became a cause celebrity. Most likely, you feel dejected, probably as a result of the heroine's short-lived high esteem. But please, I say this with no callous intent. What you did was actually negatively spirited."

"What!" He had definitely struck a tender spot.

"Bear with me. I'm begging you. I will explain exactly what I mean."

"This had better be good," she said.

"It's truth, Desiree, that we can't so easily deny. The Freedom Riders came together, joined forces to tear down, destroy an old system. This is not to say your cause was not just, it most certainly was. But the focus was on destroying, not building. The pain of destruction is what you rejected and suffered. Tearing down is essential to reform, but if one takes on a project of destroying that someone must be just as eager at rebuilding."

"How old are you, Alan?"

He chuckled. "What brought that on?"

"I want to know, so I asked." Desiree saw his mischievous grin reappear. "Don't lie, she said."

"I was born in '43, which ought to make me just about one score eight. What's my age got to do with the tint of toast?"

"Do you always talk like an old strait-laced professor lecturing a class full of truth-seekers? I am by the way, two years older than you."

"And you're smarter too. I have studied your situation because I care. I'd guess, correct me if I'm wrong, you weren't spiritually grounded when you got involved with the Freedom Riders."

"Only if I could have been grounded without being aware of it," Desiree answered.

"Chaos and recovery from death put you in touch with your spiritual self. Not knowing it, or maybe trying to deny it might have a lot to do with your affliction." Drawn closer by the alluring pull of her eyes, the Reverend read fascination as well as distrust in them. "If compared to what you endured, my struggles were inconsequential. I had some terrible bouts with my conscience for not rejecting my advisors' at school, and my Mom's appeals to not get involved in the movement for voting rights. I lost dear friends in Mississippi." Alan paused. He would bet his shirt she was infatuated but would probably resist. He must tell her anyway. "Desiree, I told my folks I would invite you to come with me for a visit. I long to see them."

"Oh no you didn't." She maneuvered to the curb, jamming the brakes to an abrupt stop. Why did he break the enchantment? Desiree sharpened her words against clenched teeth. "Without asking me? Not that it would have made any difference. Dry up and go away, right now."

"What's that supposed to mean?"

Desiree banged the palm of her hand on the steering wheel, emphasizing every word. "Your folks needn't know anything about me. How dare you! Do you think I'm that naive? Do you really think I can't see through your conniving jive?"

"Wrong, Desiree, on both counts. I want you to marry me, or I marry you. Oh what the hell, however the question is supposed to be asked."

"Why, because you feel sorry for me?"

Alan stared at her, breathing deeply.

"Well!"

He spoke softly, as he had in vespers. "I'm going home to Peterson Chapel. The official notice came yesterday. Peterson cancelled its affiliation with the AME conference, It has been declared a landmark by the Natural Registry of Historic Places. I am known there. The challenge to begin social and spiritual change is waiting for me. It is waiting for you, too. Here in Philadelphia, I will remain a very good assistant or an unemployed minister. This urbane world is actually insulted by my revelation of its spiritual self. I know though, what I must do and above all else, I will be true to myself. I gave Reverend Charles my resignation this morning."

"I thought I made myself perfectly clear last week," Desiree snapped.

"You did, and I have searched my soul for a clearer understanding of the trauma from seeing the spirit of death, as you have experienced it in its unglorified disgrace. You are the conscience of America's benevolent society. Our paths crossed for a reason, Desiree. The planning of that is beyond my ability. I am destined to be with you. Unfortunately for me, maybe us, I will drop out of your sight tomorrow, unless you reconsider my invitation to at least come visit. I'm pleading with all that I am worth for this not to be farewell, consciousness dignified."

Desiree spit the words back at him. "Consciousness dignified to your smart aleck self." His words bothered her for meaning, as she watched him get out and walk away.

#

CHAPTER 10

Hastings, NC and a Promise

Thanksgiving 1971

After Alan left town Desiree tried to take each day's ending for granted. If the sun rose it would surely set. So what? Yet, its dull red glow setting behind the Germantown hills disquieted her. The moon hadn't risen the previous night, at least she hadn't seen it. A weird overcast sky laid a disturbing concern on her heart. Desiree tried not to give the matter much thought, even as she rifled through slips of loose paper on her dresser looking for his parents' phone number. Desiree told herself she should wait at least a week. She wouldn't want her call to beat him home or plant the thought in him or his parents' minds that she was desperate. After a week, her heart's yearning began screaming.

A woman Desiree hoped was Alan's mother answered the phone.

"Hello." A gentle contralto voice sang its greeting.

Desiree opened her mouth to speak, hoping to respond in a like manner, but nothing came out.

"Hello?"

"Oh, ah, yes ma'am." Desiree sounded like a squeaking mouse. "I am Desiree Pierson calling long distance for Reverend Alan Duberry. Might this be the right number?"

"Desiree, what a pretty name. Alan said you might be calling. Just a moment."

"Thank you. It was my mother's choice, my name I mean," Desiree said, awkwardly.

"Hi," Alan piped in.

Alan piped in, disrupting the conversation. "Have you packed?"

"Alan, please!" Desiree spoke harshly, and heard the other phone disconnect. "I need a moment with your mother."

He continued rambling as if he hadn't heard her. "You are coming I believe, at least I hope. I will be one miserable cuss if you don't."

"Your mother, please give her the phone!"

"Okay, but what can she tell you that I haven't?"

"You're a dunce. Am I, a female stranger, welcome in her home for an overnight or weekend visit? You, a new male friend of mine, a stranger to my mother would never spend the night in her home."

"Even if I knelt at the altar and lifted the roof praying in her Pentecostal Church?"

"The Amos and Andy guffaw is not you, or I've been mistaken. Mrs. Duberry needs to know about me. What I, not you, want to project."

"She's never met Rosa Parks. But she'd be the highest bidder if Mrs. Parks was in Hastings and needed accommodation for whatever reason. You, like her, are a cause celebrity."

"Alan, that is downright dumb, and this is my quarter..."

"Well a, uh-oh, I'm in trouble now. Mom wants the phone."

"Desiree?" His mother spoke. "I heard everything. Come join us for Thanksgiving and stay the weekend. The National Registry granted Peterson Chapel its certificate some weeks ago. Isn't that just wonderful? Bring your mother or dad, both if you like. Need I say why I feel like I already know you?"

Desiree noted a trace of laughter. "Well, no, not really." She wondered if her voice revealed embarrassed-laced excitement. "Are you sure I, or maybe we wouldn't be a burden?"

"We'll send the menfolk to sleep in Alan's new parsonage. If you come alone, he will stay over there by himself. How about it?"

"Thanks, I'll discuss your invitation with my parents. Might I call you back in a few days?"

"Certainly, say by Thursday?"

"Thursday is fine, Mrs. Duberry. Thanks."

"Bye, Desiree. Here's Alan."

"Yeah, Desiree," he said cheerfully.

"Alan, you never did tell me how you fit into the movement."

He wondered about her reason for that inquiry. "Okay, if your decision hinges on my association. For openers, I organized a SNCC, Student Nonviolent Coordinating Committee, chapter at Sankore University.

When the Mississippi scene got real ugly, I was in the seminary working on my Divinity Degree. I wrote papers for the movement, organized a candle light vigil, and took part in the march on Washington. I will tell you all about it."

"Why not right now?"

"It's an awful lot, like years of conditioning and tough decisions, heart aches. When our paths crossed, I was just finishing my final obligation. Can it wait?"

"Well, I suppose so." Desiree had no other reason to fake resisting.

"Looking forward to your coming." Alan said.

"I'll be in touch. Goodbye."

Desiree called as she had promised, and in thanking Alicia for the invitation, said they would stay from Wednesday to Friday. During the conversation with Alan, she jokingly admitted she had lowered the barrier around her heart, and teased Alan that he had done his darndest to vault it. No denying it, she wanted a good look-see. Her folks accepting his parents' invitation would serve well in keeping Alan and them from overwhelming her. Desiree's father insisted they travel by bus.

Some weeks later, as Desiree stepped off the bus in Hastings, NC, Alan greeted her with bright smiling eyes, and clasped her hands. Desiree introduced him to Rebecca and Jimmy Pierson. Alan, awkward and stumbling over his words, made their acquaintances with Patrick and Alicia Duberry. Mrs. Duberry was exactly as Desiree had pictured her from the ring of eloquence in her voice. Brown eyes, cocoa complexioned, five foot-six, well-proportioned but showing signs of a middle-age spread. Ruddy complexioned Patrick, six feet tall with an ample physique that bespoke of intensive training earlier in his life. The years had begun rounding out his upper back. His brown eyes, with tear sacs visible under them and looking tired, expressed sincere friendliness. A gold cap on his right eyetooth befitted a handsome face. Alan drove with Desiree up front between him and her father. All six rode comfortably compacted in Patrick's '68 Chevrolet.

Observing Desiree staring out the window at the passing landscape of East Hastings, Alan explained its origin from an old hamlet that sprang from a yellow-dirt crossroads in Reconstruction times. Once a huge tobacco plantation, Hastings emerged as two boroughs, one white, the other black, on land endowed to the original slave family by the Hastings Clan. Dewey Mayfield, president of Peterson Chapel board of trustees and Sister Aida McPhearson were two descendants of that first black family. Ties of the Hastings Family included Hastings National Bank, and the First Bank and Guaranty Office in the Land Title Building. Through courthouse manipulations and taxation, the black side sank into despair, while the white side grew with the influx of industry and commerce. The Southern Railway, President Franklin Roosevelt's payback to Democrats for the States electoral votes, established a railroad boundary between the segregated communities. It lasted until black resistance to the old South threatened the facade of blacks' and whites' separate, and peaceful existence. Though the demographics remained the same, civil rights pressure on southern politics, and advice from the

Department of Housing and Urban Development on revenue sharing, resulted in the merger. One application from a combined Hastings would yield more revenue than two separate ones from East and West. In the threatening aftermath of the assassination of Reverend Martin Luther King Jr., the town council elected its first black council member, Ely J. Mulgoon. The hiring of two black police officers and placing the police department under the umbrella of civil service were worthy examples of a town striving towards racial balance. Hastings High School integrated the year Reverend Duberry went off to college.

On their way to the Duberry's home, Alicia suggested they stop by Peterson Chapel's new parsonage. In the moment, Alan swerved left off Oak Road onto Branch Pike, a state highway the locals called Ninety-One. The turn pushed Desiree up against him, making her discomfort obvious, as she struggled against her unaware father, who was occupied by observing the passing landscape.

Desiree's mother, Rebecca, had already glued her eyes on Alan, like a bird of prey after leaping salmon. Patrick, jammed against a back door, spoke in the low, biting voice of a Black North Carolinian. Alan heard his rebuke and in the rear-view mirror caught sight of a stern reproving gaze from his mother when she faked clearing her throat. He apologized for the recklessness and creeped into the driveway of a colony-gold, four-bedroom rectangular stone house with a two-car attached garage. He opened the car doors, while from the corner of his eye, observed every sensuous move Desiree made. "It is spread out over most of half of an acre." Alan gave his mother keys to the front door, and silently coaxed

Desiree to go with him out back. She went but held back expressing adulation while strolling with him among patches of blossoming wild flowers that created a natural border around the enchanted setting. A few old and very tall Southern pines the contractor had spared shaded the west side from direct rays of the sultry North Carolina sun.

Desiree sat in a gazebo with its fragrant lemon balm plant, gathering her thoughts. The house was too majestic. It made her feel uncomfortable. Alan looked at her, the question etched in his face.

"Nothing is wrong," she said. "So much... It just makes we wonder why me?"

"Me too, Desiree. If we can believe it is part of a master plan, and I do. Then we realize, for everything, there is a reason. Accepting this gift, means that we honor its obligation."

"Yoo-hoo, Alan and Desiree." Alicia's call broke their interlude.

Brimming with pride, they joined the others in a contemporary styled kitchen.

"It is a designer's work of art," Desiree exclaimed, though she didn't like the living and dining room windows. They were dressed in lavender velvet drapes and daffodil curtains, which shut out the sunlight and blocked view of the magnolia. Its dark Victorian furniture forced an annoying gloom reminiscent of a funeral parlor.

She and the Reverend would have to replace the window dressings, Alicia stated with a wink at her son, indicating that it was a matter of taste that reflected personalities. Patrick, bored with the nonsensical conversation, wondered aloud if curtains were worthy reasons to wait dinner. His concern having resonated well, they piled into the car and left.

On Oak Road just beyond the town boundary, Reverend Duberry turned onto a yellow dirt driveway beside his parents' home. They had built the ranch style bungalow on an acre of ground after moving from East Hastings some years before the East-West merger. They called it a two-fold blessing of the civil rights crusade. The First State Bank of Hastings had just begun mortgaging long-awaited FHA approved homes for African Americans. Patrick's high score on the civil service exam, and having been awarded extra points for military service, afforded him an opportunity to quit the sawmill. He worked in a quiet and air-conditioned post office.

On the front porch two wicker rocking chairs sat side by side in the partial shade of a Magnolia tree. Inside, the antique décor and cozy ambiance further melted Desiree's surface apprehension. Walls in the hallway that extended back to the kitchen were cedar paneled. In the living room, concentric circles of a braided wool rug, and white curtains with soft-yellow ruffled bordering, supported indications of a happy home. They were pulled back at two front windows, and neatly tied with big white and yellow bows. An upright piano occupied the same corner it had since the day Reverend Duberry, his mother, and father had moved into the new home. A gilt brass floor lamp older than the Reverend stood beside it. Mrs. Duberry had placed two walnut end tables, and a coffee table beside and in front of a flower-print cloth sofa. A family portrait was mounted at eye level on each side of the fireplace. On the left hung the picture of Alicia Arnold's and Patrick Duberry's nuptial at her rural home in Brown's Mountain, near Knoxville, Tennessee. On the right were pictures of the Reverend, a toddler with his parents in the old East Hastings home. Desiree asked about the other photographs occupying the remaining wall space. Alan explained the photographs of his grand, great, and great-great paternal and maternal grandparents. Some dated back to the days when Hastings was a plantation, and Brown's Mountain was an isolated community in the foothills of the Great Smoky Mountains.

After supper, Desiree and Alan walked into town, though it was more like a country hike for a Philadelphia city girl, along a country landscape on a chilly moonlit night. Strolling Oak Avenue past Peterson Chapel, Alan beamed with confidence, explaining the possibilities he envisioned. He touched her wrist, slid his fingers slowly over it and firmly grasped Desiree's hand. Her fingers squealed delightfully in the heat of his tender clasp. They slurped root beer floats and giggled at each other in Doc Whitlow's ice cream parlor and pharmacy. In Cootie's night club, a ways down Martin Luther King Way, a rhythm and blues house-rocking band livened an otherwise quiet night. Alan and Desiree wandered in the opposite direction to the Community Center Park.

"Right here could be the beginning of a new era. The phantom my mind is pursuing... Oh, Desiree." He mixed his thoughts, talking rapidly. "I am feeling so powerful and happy. There is nothing in my vision I can't do, that is if you would marry me."

Desiree stopped walking and slowly, but firmly removed her hands from his.

"Don't say anything just yet," he said. "Hear me first. I have imagined this several times and offered it up in prayer to the Almighty. Each time I see you, like tonight in the moonlight."

"And what am I doing?" Her voice a husky whisper.

"Descending the stairway from the stars, coming to be with me. If you say yes, I will work at establishing a center for social awareness, and name it after Martin Luther King, Jr. A challenge to enrich the soul of America with the two of us sustaining each other in a holistic lifestyle. We can do it."

Though she did not answer, Desire's entire being glowed.

He waited. Anticipating her reply made him embarrassingly self-conscious. "Well, uh it's quite a walk back home. I'll ask Dad or Mom, whoever answers the phone to come get us."

"Let's walk." Desiree took his hand. He nodded and let her lead the way. They walked some distance in silence, inching closer until his arm encircled her narrow waist. Her head lay against his upper arm. "Alan?"

"Uh-hunh?"

Desiree whispered "You know there can be no children, and I haven't known you long enough. Haven't had time to let myself confide in your word. But supposing I will?"

Alan exhaled a long releasing sigh of anxiety. "At least it is something for me to hang my promise on. Some of the most adorable, orphaned babies in the world are begging for someone to love them." He turned and kissed her hair. Desire wheeled and embraced him tightly. On her tiptoes, she pressed opened lips to his. Her kiss sang through his veins. Desiree pulled away, her mouth burning with desire. They walked on, imagination-laced wanting coursing through Alan like molten lava down a mountainside. Desiree wanted to know his thoughts but was too on guard for what his response would likely be, and not sure she could resist. Finally, after listening to her breathing synchronized with his, and feeling her body and his sway and stride in harmony, she couldn't resist any longer. "A penny for your thoughts."

"You already know mine. It's on you."

"Yes. Like right now."

Alan entered the house behind Desiree bubbling with pride and singing, "We're getting married in the morning."

"Down here or up home in Philly," Desiree's father blurted.

"Hush, Jimmy, and take your medicine," Desiree's mother scolded as she handed him the vial of hypertension medicine. "We're going to do it up just right in Philadelphia."

"It needn't be anything elaborate, Mom." Desiree said.

"Good news," Alicia said, joyfully. "Now that we have a plan working, night-night gents, off to the parsonage. And Patrick, don't forget your blood pressure pill."

"Who'll remind you of yours?" Patrick laughed heartily and stretched up from his easy chair. "Tell you right now, mates, I eat, but I don't do breakfast."

"C'mon back over here for waffles and sausage," Alicia said. "We don't want hot grease splattered all over the church's brand-new kitchen."

"Son." Patrick cast a teasing eye at Desiree. "Might we take Desiree along for a late-night sampling of her culinary skills?"

"Jimmy, your stomach is way too tired and timid for midnight snacking, especially on Thanksgiving eve," Rebecca teased.

"Desiree stays with us, and once again," Alicia said. "Goodnight!"

"I'm just trying to find out how Alan's go'n get some meat on his lanky bones." Patrick said.

Desiree noted Patrick's devilish eyes dancing. "Mister Duberry, if you can handle my kind of holistic cooking, say like bean sprouts and tofu, I'll gladly cook you a meal, but not tomorrow's."

Jimmy roared with laughter. "Better be careful of what you ask for, old Dude."

"Actually." A broad smile stretched across Alan's face. "Desiree and I are going to pick up where Martin Luther King left off."

"And do what?" Patrick's voice had a critical tone.

"Not his banner, *We Shall Overcome,* but with a different attack on America's social diseases, beginning right here in Hastings."

"At Peterson, Alan?"

"Sure, Mom, but no marching or protesting."

"And Desiree?"

"She will teach yoga and meditation."

"Desiree can do it, all right. Lord knows she made me see the light." Jimmy dabbed his eyes with a handkerchief. "But Alan, I gotta tell ya'ain't much in tofu and wheat grass that'll put meat on your bones."

While they laughed, Desiree's mother cried softly. "Hallelujah." Rebecca waved a hand over her head. "Thank you Jesus. You have seen me through tears and dread, praying for my baby, a lamb such as yourself on Calvary."

Desiree only listened; despite being caught unexpectedly in a situation that demanded she say something. Whatever she might say though, would bring on more of her mother's lamenting and her father begging forgiveness. She offered a tender smile, which had become habitual to their worn rhetoric.

Alan, sensing her discomfort, cleared his throat. "Flowers of sacrifice have bloomed this lunar year."

"Say what, Son?" Patrick asked.

"It is spiritual significance appropriate for Desiree. Flowers nurture the soul. Desiree is the bouquet. That's all I need say."

"Alan." Alicia's warm voice sang. "You are blushing."

"Aww, Mom." He looked askance. "Actually, I have believed since my undergrad days at school that I could find a way to eradicate racism and sexism in America. I committed myself to work hard at it, and that it would probably take a long time. It didn't take long to realize the size of such a task, and that I couldn't do it alone. Desiree and I will make it our souls' experience. We hope the response will have a ripple effect, like rain drops in a pool of water; first ten, then a hundred, thousands, millions."

"That is one hell of a commitment for a spanking brand-new couple not even having chance to know each other yet," Patrick said.

Alan though, didn't swallow his dad's hook for a verbal duel. He and Desiree retreated, with sweaters on, to the Gazebo in the back yard. He began slowly rocking the glider. Desiree, planting her feet firmly on the wood flooring, stopped it.

"Alan, everything I have seen in my short time here is inviting. Now I need time to put all of it in a perspective that assures me I can fit in. Let's slow down. You promised to tell me more about your Dad and Mom."

"Yes, I did. Dad?" he called out. "You and Mr. Pierson go on over to the parsonage. Mom, can I use your car after a while? We're going to sit a spell."

Alan adjusted the pillows on the glider and leaning back, he stared into the night, deciding where to begin discussing his father. Entwining his fingers with Desiree's he slowly rocked. "Dad's roots run deep in Hastings. When I came along he was a bitter man, but through his long, tortuous nights, he always loved Mom and me. On the strength of that, she endured until he came out of it."

Desiree laid her head on Alan's shoulder and murmured softly. "Tell me more."

#

CHAPTER 11

A Black Father Speaks of Coping

No dateline

Patrick Duberry's rugged stance against racism provided the protective wing under which Alan walked the segregated streets of Hastings among his peers with a dignified black pride. He was not a naïve black youngster taking life for granted. During Alan's last summer before going away to school, he became closer to his Dad than he had been since he was ten years old.

It came about one sultry July night, a couple hours after darkness had settled. Alan, swaying in a glider on the back porch, had been contemplating college, his entanglement in local civil rights struggles, and his years not really knowing his father. The spontaneous connections in mind of those events were abruptly suspended by a peal of laughter. That, and his father's fiery red pipe glowing in darkness, intensified

Alan's urge to engage him in affable conversation. He went and stood outside of a netted tent-house.

"Dad?"

"Hey," Patrick replied. "Come in on the safe side, away from the bugs and sit down."

"Just want to say I appreciate all you did," Alan said, unzipping the flap. "The sacrifices made so this day would come for me."

Patrick rubbed his palms together and spoke slowly. "When I look back over your life," he said, halting and drawing on his pipe, "it's like you might say, wandering through the pages of a history book." He waved his hands in front of his face, searching for words to adequately express himself. "Or better yet, a historical take on Alan Warren Duberry, compiled and edited by Patrick and Alicia Duberry. It'd be a real good read, son."

"I'd like to hear it, Dad, your overall picture of me."

"Why don't you get us a couple cokes? See if Alicia can join us."

Mrs. Duberry readily accepted.

Waiting for them to join him, Alan's father searched himself again, making sure he could, in a conciliatory though frank way, slip the hasp off an aspect of himself long overdue. Definitely, he must broach it before Alan's mindset stretched too far beyond his reach. In that reckoning, Patrick had come to understand that he was driven by a conscience of love, fighting to express itself in an ego-driven man. A civil rights black father whose capacity to love had been shaped by his environment, and by mentors who demanded that he love Jesus, but said little about loving himself.

That had caused problems for a young Patrick, but he nursed his rejection silently to avoid excruciating pain to his behind. Telling his son about it, Patrick called it pre-civil rights madness. Patrick readily admitted that his wife and son taught him how to love by doing it.

"You know." He laughed heartily as Alicia and Alan stepped into the tent. "We black folks in America don't know how badly we have been cheated out of our heritage. We are still too damned occupied with problems of predestination, like the origin of evil and original sin. But neither one never amounted to much more than a hill of beans when compared to our true culture, our lineage and legacies."

Gushes of exhaled air stoked his pipe, as Patrick intoned about longing to know what was on the other side of the darkness beyond death. He called it an awful task that forced people his age to learn how, and then examine the worthiness of life. "But with all that examining we still can't understand the genetic loading of our ancestral parenthood for a sound explanation of our African collective consciousness. Know what I'm driving at, son?"

"Afraid I don't, Dad."

"Then look at it this way. Our genetic memory, in other words, our hereditary identification with our ancestors is a sub-conscious library of who we are." Patrick hesitated, waiting for an amazed reaction from Alan, and then he stole a side-glance at Alicia. "Take that off to college with you, son, and come back with some answers. I am as serious as death."

His wife sat as stone-faced as a statue observing him, while his son anxiously listened for more, hearing seldom-expressed insight.

"Wow, Dad. I will. You promised a couple minutes ago to tell me how the earlier civil rights years impacted my life."

"Oh, yeah, I did, didn't I?"

Alan had come along in '43, a cataclysmic year, Patrick told his son, as well as a paradoxical one. After World War II, it was a time for turning away from weapons of mass destruction, but also a time becoming increasingly symbolic of death actually defying life. In that year, the separate but equal doctrine of Holy Willie the hypocrite and Jim Crow his enforcer, were finally recognized and labeled for what they really were; two bastard stepsons of the Supremacist. Holy Willie, a white pathetic liar, spit venomous deceit from both sides of his crooked mouth. His brother Jim, crude, mixed black and white, and mentally deficient, stood in mocked conceit at toilet doors, and foul-smelling water fountains, waving *Whites Only* and *Coloreds* flags. Together, Willie and Jim, the crippling American consciousness, worked an imperialism no less vicious than Fuehrer Hitler's, Dictator Mussolini's, or Emperor Hirohito's. That consciousness practically held the entire nation in check until the heroic Tuskegee fighter pilots, Buffalo Soldiers, Black Marines, and the Seamen began returning home from overseas. These angry, and valorous men reappearing from foreign battlefields— Normandy, Salerno, Pearl Harbor, Seoul, and Da Nang—locked horns with Holy Willie and Jim Crow. The double V, a symbol for victory on the battlefield, became the recognition of brotherhood among many black and white returning warriors. Patrick taught it to Alan before the little fellow could clearly pronounce his name. He helped organize a local interracial chapter of the American Veterans Committee. Hastings was first in the South to establish an American Veterans chapter, his segregated hometown's first attempt at integration.

"I could do with another coke." Patrick burped. "S'cuse me."

"Me too, I'll get a couple. What about you, Mom? Wait until I get back, Dad."

"One's plenty for me." Alicia stepped out of the tent behind their son, and zipped up the flap.

"Sleep is coming on fast." She lied. Patrick's need to vent harbored guilt was a man's thing between father and son.

"Alicia," Patrick called to her, "didn't we save a few of them baby back ribs from supper? Oops, s'cuse me again, dear. Stomach just growled. Chewing the rag in this night air worked up a little appetite."

She continued a slow stroll to the steps leading to the back porch, then turned. "Eating pork at this hour Patrick, on your sour belly? You need Pepto Bismol, but I'll make the sandwich." Alicia appreciated Patrick making sure she was beyond earshot before he continued his spiel.

Alan simply chuckled.

Patrick had come home from Navy combat in the South Pacific Theater to his old dead-end job at the Sawmill. He began yielding to an anger and booze laced depression. His entrance examination scores had earned him promised admittance to the Naval Academy at Annapolis. Instead, he was ordered to the Frogs and worse yet, classified as a cook; manipulations that essentially denied him all probabilities of a career as a US Naval ensign.

"Wait a minute, Dad." Alan interrupted Patrick's recollecting. "You actually cooked and didn't..."

"I did some cooking. That was my classification."

"You weren't supposed to tell us you were a Frog?"

"In the record, son, I am listed as a cook."

When Patrick came home, he drank just a little too much on weekends. It began on Friday after work, and then splashed over to a couple of heavy jolts on stormy Monday mornings. Monday's jolts soothed the mad dog's bite from Sunday. Before long, Tuesdays became chasing the blues days—fighting depression—sometimes for lunch or after work at home. Wednesday nights at the Colored Vets' Home, reliving war and Holy Willie experiences brought on intense bouts of anger that only more of the jug would cap. Thursday morning slugs usually quieted the former night's fire. Friday came again.

Often, the new week required more liquor than the last. Before long, no excuses were given, none requested. The hard drinking didn't turn son away from father, as much as the cold loneliness in Patrick's dead-pan expression. It froze his son at a distance, depriving him of companionship. During some weekend bouts, the edge of the bed was his bar stool. Though the youngster didn't tell Patrick, those war stories instilled in him a pride for his father that nothing could shake loose.

Patrick's feeble, amusing attempts never fooled Alan. The inquisitive lad's sincere and caring stare forced his father to admit truthfully that a den of weird snakes hadn't made him quit.

"Truth is, Son, Grandma Nana Cleo's ghost came one night, and smacked me sober. 'You don't want me to come again. Get up and bathe your breathe. Don't lay beside your wife another night stinking like all be gone to hell!'"

Patrick sat on the bed's edge drenched in sweat, rubbing his cheeks, and admitting to himself that he must have struck rock-bottom to have earned Nana Cleo's wrath. Alicia had gone into the guest bedroom, like she often did when his binge became unbearable.

Patrick began spending hours in solitude, browsing books that forced him to look hard at himself, and reading recent ones Alicia bought for Alan on black boyhood. Choosing to spend time with favorite poets, reading autobiographies and philosophical content on the meaning of blackness in America, Patrick learned what he could best accomplish by assenting to a shameful past. He had considered a writing career before grand promises from the Navy routed that idea from his mind. Melvin B. Tolson, a poet and professor Patrick had met many years ago at a summer internship at Lincoln University, had written a poetic articulation in his book, *The Curator,* which Patrick accepted for his own confession:

Black Boy, the vineyard is the fittest place in which to booze with Omar (Persian Poet) and study soil and time and integrity—the telltale triad of grape and race."

Reflecting on his past with Tolson's insight and memorizing much of it, Patrick elevated himself into a respectful groove where he identified with a bag of literary and musical giants—Bontemps, Wright, Hurston, Dizzy, Bird, Powell, Jean Tomer. But more so than digging these new friends' gifts and prophecies for the therapeutic necessity of it, Patrick grew to trust his judgment on how he had been manipulated, and why he had been so deceived. Yes, there had been plenty of pain. Alicia, whom he loved dearly, at times seemed to understand. But then, there were the other times. Yet, while he grappled with the uncertainties of his change, as far as he could tell, she never considered any other choices other than to wait.

"Alan." She called out from a screened kitchen door. "Come get your dad's sandwich." Hearing brief snatches of rapt with Alan, she had piled on several thick slices of Bermuda onion and a cherry pepper.

"Okay, Mom. Wow. Dad will be talking all night."

#

CHAPTER 12

Alicia, an Exemplary Expression of Mother Wit

No dateline

Perseverance and hope, like black-eyed peas and cornbread, Alicia believed it would replenish the depleted marrow in her bones. She needed a recharge, and knew her son had become aware, at least from a child's perspective, of her burden. Taking him with her from Hastings across the mountains into Tennessee, she noted his inquisitive looks. She simply told him they were going back home to Brown Mountain for a few days to check on Gammy and Pop-pop. There in the sanctity of their log-cabin bungalow, in that Great Smoky Mountain community of Colored folk, Alicia Arnold-Duberry would unload her burden. A black woman grappling with the madness of Black American manhood resisting the trampling boots of Holy Willie and Jim Crow.

Alicia relied on her mother, a little bespectacled and brown complexioned lady with greying hair, and her father. He, dark-hued and razor-thin, would help replenish her emotional state. In that beguiling setting, Alicia absorbed herself in its hypnotic stillness, while Alan and his grandparents entertained each other. Through inner acting, Alicia's parents could assess the condition of mother and son.

A couple mornings after Alicia had unloaded her burden, she and Gammy dived into the task of finding resolve to her situation.

"Is the determination to save to your marriage, and fear that Alan might gravitate toward his father breaking you down?"

'Well, if that is what you see in me. But my concern runs deeper than saving my marriage.

"Alicia! You can't mean that?"

"I do, Mom. Definitely. Patrick is one in a group of ambitious and otherwise brilliant and ambitious black men who were driven to despair by institutionalized racism in the U S Navy. That major influence sustained in him self-pity in one respect, and in the other a perverted black male pride. Both drove him to drink, and now it is out of control. I understand that."

"Yes, I can, too." Gammy said

"What I don't understand is why it drives them to challenge liquor so relentlessly. Why it drives them to outdo their white counterparts, despite not being recognized. Why do they ridicule anyone among them who can't compete at their level? Black men who can't function in that mindset, or can't win the challenges, are held in contempt. The contempt is more vicious than their hatred for whites in the military, who denied men of Patrick's caliber the dignity of superior achievement.

And worse, Patrick won't accept the damaging division creeping in between him and Alan."

"Obviously, that is the main cause of your distress, right?"

"Yes. His denial quashes the shame. We don't talk about it, except to admit that it is a mysterious cycle that seals the lips of fathers and of boys destined to become fathers. I have discussed this with similar distraught women."

"Alicia." Her father called from outside. "Alan's found a playmate. Sitting here alone, I couldn't help overhearing." He came in from a breezeway and stood in the doorway. "Try to imagine any honorable black father telling his son that second best ain't worth one hot damn, but Holy Willie still go'n deny him his top credits. Can you?"

"I have already tried, Dad."

"You and a million others. Alcohol quiets the beast only for the moment. Their addiction in this no-win battle is destroying young black minds. We need a new strategy."

"We mustn't blame them." Desiree's mother said.

"But they must bear the responsibility," Pop-pop said, or wallow in the cruel cycle until..."

"Until? Until what?" Alan said, while Gammy tried to signal by partially covering her finger pointing to the floor, that Alan stood behind his grandfather listening.

"I won't dwell on the down side." He turned and laughed at his grandson standing behind him, absorbing every word. "If he is smart enough to understand, let him hear. Some brave folks among us have made history battling Holy Willie way back since slavery. Ida B. Wells for one. Born a slave, she was a journalist, a publisher, and started the anti-lynching movement.

"Yep. My father kept stacks of her newspaper until they turned to dust. But, Pop-pop, this is not suitable talk for a seven-year-old." Alicia's mother cautioned him.

"Let's not pretend he doesn't know."

"He will ask until his little inquisitive mind is satisfied." Alicia laughed heartily.

"Now, we need lots of voices," her father said, "demanding decency together, like the Durham Manifesto. It discussed lynching from a depth of feeling concerned whites could actually sense the fear and anger. I saved several write-ups on it." He bent down and affectionately rubbed his grandson's head.

After several days of reaffirming her commitment to marriage, and accepting her son as a source of inspiration, Alicia bid her parents a thankful good-bye. On their way home Alan asked in happenstance conversation, about Columbus discovering America. Good for him that she taught school and was adept at separating fact from fiction. Her story was different than the one taught in American history books.

In December 1955, West Hastings Elementary School was integrated, and Mrs. Rosa Parks refused a white man her seat on a bus in Montgomery, Alabama. Holy Willie couldn't bring himself to believe she actually possessed the courage to defy Jim Crow. While Willie ranted that she was a Communist—a secret agent from the Kremlin—Mrs.

Parks hoisted the flag of revolution, from which sprang the prominence of African American womanhood. Out of the shock wave she generated, the Reverend Martin Luther King, Jr emerged. Alicia lost her job, a result of the rift caused by resentful white backlash to forced integration of public schools.

When Alan became fourteen, Peterson Chapel Sunday School selected him, a student with a powerful mind, as one of three delegates to its annual Sunday school convention. Alicia's closest friend, Mrs. Gyce, the youngsters' chaperone, suggested Alan address the conference. She was confident he would do well and attract attention as a future leader in the church. With a teenager's unbridled truthfulness, he challenged the conference with a recommendation that sent shock waves reverberating back to Hastings, North Carolina.

"Instead of chasing the Horatio Alger dream, Peterson Chapel should urge the Church Conference to send some historians, Bible scholars, and writers to explore the ancient ruins of Egypt," he recited. "They'd uncover Africa's lost philosophy of life. There, secreted among the temples, in cities more eternal than Rome, is evidence of our fathers' living proof of life everlasting."

The chaperone wore a big secretive grin for the balance of their stay, despite the reverberations that rebounded from the clergy hierarchy. He was, nonetheless, congratulated for his novel presentation. Strange though, that no one questioned the rising young scholar until he returned home.

"What's our son been reading? At fourteen, it's impossible for him to understand what he was talking about," her husband warned.

"Our son has the mind of a young idealist," Alicia replied.

"Y'all driving him too fast for his juvenile britches."

Her son chimed in. "Read it in books Mom and Mrs. Gyce gave me."

"And?"

"And?" his father's bass voice rang out.

"And what?" Alan's firm voice carried more than a hint of disrespectful irritation.

"And you won't run from it," Alicia said, defusing him. "You will challenge yourself to make it happen if you believe, or to change it if you don't believe. That's the mark of an idealist. But remember, a title is nothing more than a label, or a simple way to tag you by someone who doesn't like you or know what you are doing." Alicia had thoroughly deflated her son. She often did that, weave in and out of his busy, inquisitive, and at times, arrogant mind. Not knowing what to say, he would shut up and listen, at least until the next time.

One April afternoon, several months after four freshmen at North Carolina's Agriculture and Technical College in Greensboro had launched a tidal wave of passive resistance, Alicia called and left Patrick a message at the post office. Their son and one hundred or so students, including some whites, were marching from Hastings High down Western Avenue, to integrate downtown Hastings. A teacher called and warned Alicia, the police had already set up a roadblock.

Though Alicia knew sit-ins were a growing protest movement by determined and courageous youth all over America, she was not prepared for the terrifying scene. She and her confidant joined other concerned parents at the intersection of Western Avenue and Jesse Helms Boulevard. The students came, marching four abreast and loudly chanting, "If we can't no one will. First class or bust." In the next block, in front of the police station, the force waited in full riot gear. Ranking officers walked among them, barking instructions. Alicia's group with other adults who had happened by, fanned out the width of the street and, made themselves a wall between the police and students. "Young people, you have made your point. Now leave the rest to us," Mrs. Gyce, the chosen leader, advised. The students stopped, but stood their ground, even when ordered by the approaching police captain to disperse for their own safety. Several terse minutes passed.

Not finding Alicia at home, Patrick had changed into his old Navy fatigues that she had neatly packed away. After dressing in the dark blue jersey and wool cap, he beat a hasty trail to downtown, but ran into a roadblock. Traffic had been detoured. He parked around a corner and hurried on toward the cordoned confrontation area. Patrick couldn't see, but he heard the captain repeat his command.

The riot police moved forward, one slow and deliberate step forward, followed by another. Alicia and her tide of women folk stood firm, facing them. Seeing the police ready for immediate confrontation, and the students move stealthily up behind the grownups, Patrick ran into the fray, confronted his son.

"Alan, and the rest of you all, back off, gawddammit, and listen. They itching to whip you-all's heads. If they do, ain't much go'n be done about it. But if your Mom and these older people get hurt, you'd rather go to hell than take the kinda' ass whupping I'm a give you.

Ashley Pitts, a dapper young black lawyer, elbowed in beside Alicia's husband, and yelled to the students that their voices had been heard. He had been in touch with Mayor Ross and was assured an answer to their grievances.

Alicia, Patrick, and Pitts and some other adults suggested they meet with the young protesters in the basement of Peterson Chapel.

Meanwhile, atop the hill in Hastings' swank country club, Mayor Stewart Ross, Police Chief Pete Davis, and Fire Marshall Ed Fabian were in closed session with the several members of Hastings Chamber of Commerce and business persons, wrestling with protest consequences. Their options were few; unconditional removal of restrictions, or face a riot, all present accepted the absolute of that. They would not tolerate a riot, but neither were they of a collective mind to give, especially young Blacks, carte blanche to roam Hastings like white folk. That was not their objective, Woolworth's manager cautioned, as the discussion continued.

At Peterson, the students vowed to blockade downtown Hastings, if racist practices persisted. If arrested, they would contact CORE, The Congress On Racial Equality.

Hearing that, Pitts hastened a second call to Mayor Ross. Speaking slowly, Pitts beseeched him, not mentioning the CORE threat, to announce an official moratorium, a five-day cooling off period. That strategy would probably stave off a riot—possibly a race riot, and discourage outside agitation from the KKK, an FBI investigation, and anyone else anxious for a new battleground. Hastings had better address this problem, Pitts said. Ross agreed and announced the moratorium. Accolades, though with trepidation and not without warnings, were extended from many persons to the students for a peaceful demonstration.

Later that evening at home sitting alone with her thoughts, Alicia longed to converse with her husband, but he seemed too drawn into himself. Addressing him in a manner that would urge him to chat, she said with a sigh, "It is hard to know how dangerous a situation really is until you are in the midst of it."

"Whose dumb idea got you all sandwiched between the kids and the police?"

"They are our babies from now until eternity. We chose to go the distance."

"It could have been real ugly. Give luck some credit. You all need to understand, fighting racism is psychological warfare. You got to strategize."

"I wonder what our son really think of us, now."

"Ask him."

"I mean, what do they say to each other?"

"He will tell you that, too, if you demand it."

Alan's approach interrupted his father's playful, yet serious rhetoric. Confident the protest movement had won his parents' supportive ears, he felt anxious to tell them what prompted his group to act on what he called a radical Black philosophy.

"What does it mean? Philosophy means it is a way of life."

"It is a grassroots weapon to fight racism, Mom." Earlier when he had approached his mother on any radical movement, Alicia told him fear of innocent bloodshed had vexed her spirits about it.

Having recently studied Socrates, *Apology*, it was the literary force that inspired Alan to explore his new philosophy. "I, you, Dad, none of us, have the right to condemn another person's action unless we can offer something better."

"Oh really now, that is quite a broad statement," Alicia said. "I don't think it would apply to any and everything."

"Can't disagree with it though," her husband countered. "It is a sound argument."

"Our march today was to start a movement. We need some heavyweight radicals to come here. Help us turn Hastings upside down."

"Today's march was bad. Who do you have in mind? If you're worried about the Klan, don't, tonight, tomorrow or ever." Words impatiently spilled from Patrick's mouth. "Me, by myself, at my age and without comrades, guys I know would help if I asked, could take out Hastings without support of bungling amateurs. But we are beyond that!"

Alicia seized the opportunity to defuse Alan's electrified energy and Patrick's heavy artillery rejection. "I can offer something better, Alan. So, I have earned the right to condemn your action, or whatever you call it, right?"

He wouldn't be disrespectable. "Yes'm, Mom." A deflated sigh eked from his nostrils.

"Now," she said, hesitating for strict attention. "Giving Socrates credit for scientific argument was a good one, but I can offer something better." She handed him a book.

"*Stolen Legacy*, by George G.M. James. *Greek Philosophy Is Stolen Egyptian Philosophy?*" He leafed hurriedly through its table of contents until his eyes focused on a sub-heading: *The Egyptian theory of salvation became the purpose of Greek philosophy.*

"Thanks, but why are you giving this to me now?"

"I think you're just about ready for it. Before you begin philosophizing about revolutions, read it until you thoroughly understand."

"Mom, you always manage to work some home-spun gimmick on me."

"I'm trying to keep your promise to God from withering into a fool's pipe dream."

Alan frowned. "I promised God something that could become a pipe-dream?"

"A pipe-dream is a promise without a conscience, a mouthful of hot air especially when you're acting silly." She narrowed her eyes on Alan.

"I don't think I'm being silly one bit, Mom."

"Well then, how easy the young mind full of pharaohs and revolution forgets," Alicia said. "Some summers ago, the Sunday School convention at New Sankore. Egypt, remember? And I didn't say you promised God a pipe-dream."

Alan stole a sidelong glance at Patrick that painfully assured him there'd be no support coming from his father.

"CORE and SNCC are fine organizations in the struggle against imperialism. But didn't we prove today that we are capable of keeping the movement alive here, Son? When the novelty wears off activist ideology," Alicia continued. "When the voices become bleaker than howling winds in the cold wilderness, we will need leaders to help the unfortunate who can't grasp the new ideology. Trailblazers without guns to see the struggle to fruition. If not you, then who? That's destiny beckoning. In case you've forgotten, I'm reminding you."

#

CHAPTER 13

Goodnight, Alan

November 1971

Alan rubbed his tired, dry lips, and gently moved his shoulder. "If I don't forge a path to total equality, chances are good that it will inflict an emotional scar on my mother's battle-weary heart."

Desiree stirred. "The moratorium," she asked. "Did it last five days?"

"I sipped a coke in Woolworth's the next day." Alan tilted her face up to his, for a scrumptious kiss.

"And it's about time you headed on over to the parsonage," Alicia teased, opening the screen door for Desiree. "Sweet dreams."

The End

Epilogue

*We take leave of Desiree. Close her journal as it were, while
she tends to wedding plans and the necessities involved
in relocating to a small Southern town. Should she worry
about whether the chance she is taking with Alan—Reverend Duberry – will be a beneficial one? He is an intelligent
and ambitious young Black minister who seethes with black
rage and acquires wisdom from black scholars more so than
simply securing knowledge of the Americana from books.
The movement impacts his life, shapes him into a crusader,
determined to make the Promised Land a reality for black
and other underprivileged persons. Desiree's yoga gifts will
be as much an integral part of their exposure to the myth of
white supremacy as the forbidden truths Alan finds in the
ancient Egyptian Mysteries.*

www.ingramcontent.com/pod-product-compliance
Lightning Source LLC
Chambersburg PA
CBHW031301060726

47590CB00003B/1013